Have you ever wondered what your parents were like at your age?

Daisy's about to find out, literally!

Be transported with Daisy to 1985. The hair! The fashion! Yikes.

Daisy's got a chance to change her future—should she take it?

What would you do differently if you could turn

Hi there!

Have you ever wished you could turn back the clock and change something you did an hour ago, last week, six months ago? Or perhaps you would like to go back and stop something from happening to you in the first place. I know I would! I've had plenty of embarrassing situations over the years that I could well do without - and no, I am NOT telling you what any of them were. You have to trust me that they were MORTIFYING!

In Back in the Day, Daisy, along with her ex-best friend, Izzy, is transported through a time portal in the school PE cupboard to 1985. It is the year their mums were at the very same school, the exact same age they are now: thirteen. Izzy wants to escape right back to their own time to avoid altering history, but Daisy has other plans. You see, Daisy's mum was killed in a car

CRASH WHEN SHE WAS FOUR AND DAISY BARELY REMEMBERS HER. THIS IS HER CHANCE TO WARN HER MUM ABOUT THE ACCIDENT, BUT BY DOING SO DAISY AND IZZY MIGHT NOT EXIST IN THE FUTURE.

WHAT WOULD YOU DO? I KNOW I WOULD TRY EVERYTHING TO KEEP MY MUM ALIVE, BUT RISKING YOUR OWN EXISTENCE IS A TRICKY ONE. CAN DAISY PULL IT OFF SO THAT SHE STILL EXISTS AND HER MUM IS ALIVE AT THE SAME TIME? SECOND CHANCES DON'T COME OFTEN IN LIFE, SO KEEP THAT IN MIND NEXT TIME YOU GET ONE AND GRAB IT WITH BOTH HANDS, LIKE DAISY DOES!

Love Jess x

I would like to dedicate this book to my husband, Neil (Saint Neil).
Thanks for always being there; your support is
much appreciated. Sorry there were no
helicopter crashes!
Lots of love x

OXFORD
UNIVERSITY PRESS

Great Clarendon Street, Oxford OX2 6DP
Oxford University Press is a department of the University of Oxford.
It furthers the University's objective of excellence in research, scholarship,
and education by publishing worldwide. Oxford is a registered trade mark of
Oxford University Press in the UK and in certain other countries

Database right Oxford University Press (maker)

First published 2016

British Library Cataloguing in Publication Data
Data available

ISBN: 978-0-19-274483-8

1 3 5 7 9 10 8 6 4 2
Printed in Great Britain

Paper used in the production of this book is a natural,
recyclable product made from wood grown in sustainable forests.
The manufacturing process conforms to the environmental
regulations of the country of origin.

BACK IN THE DAY

JESS BRIGHT

OXFORD
UNIVERSITY PRESS

Chapter One
Separate Lives

Don't you just love an argument for breakfast? It's *way* better than scrambled egg on toast or a cinnamon bagel. There I was, minding my own business, slurping my tea, when Dad breezed into the kitchen, whistling in a false Disney film over-bright manner, alerting me immediately that something was afoot . . .

'I wanted to have a little chat with you, about holidays . . .' My ears pricked up hopefully. 'I thought we could go away on holiday with Mary and her kids?'

'*What?*'

'Well, I was thinking that it might be nice, a good chance for everyone to get to know each other if we all went away for a week somewhere. Center Parcs, something like that.' I couldn't get a sound out because I was screaming inside my head.

Yes, Dad had met someone through work ten months ago ending nine years of being on the shelf after Mum had died—it had been the longest ten months of my life! I mean, how many times can I smile politely and say I don't want to go out to Pizza Express without looking like a total whingebag? I wasn't interested in making friends; who knew how long Mary would be hanging around? It didn't seem worth it! I just wanted everything to stay the same as it was before.

'I haven't mentioned it to Mary yet,' Dad said in a steady voice. 'I wanted to see what you thought first.'

'Dad, no way. Why can't we just go on our own like the last time we went to Spain?'

'Because I thought it would be fun for all of us to go. Maybe just a long weekend would be better?'

'How about nothing would be better? I'd rather not go on holiday at all.'

Dad looked at me and took a deep breath.

'Daisy, when are you going to realize I like Mary a lot. I'd like to go on holiday with her *and* with you. Just give her a chance.'

'I don't want to give her a chance. Ever! I don't want her here all the time, with Ben and Elizabeth getting in the way. I don't need her.' Yes—she had kids; Ben was six and Elizabeth was eight – just grrrrrrreat then! Elizabeth was keen on being BFFs – urgh!

'I'm not saying you do need her.'

'It's like you're trying to replace Mum.' The tea I'd

1

just drunk started swilling around in my tummy, making me feel sick. 'I don't want another mum.'

'Daisy! I'm just talking about a holiday. There's no way I would ever try and replace your mum.'

'Good, because no one will ever be as amazing as her, especially not Mary.' U-oh, I could feel a red mist descending over my head. I tried to swallow back down the words I could feel were waiting to spring.

'Daisy, we've been over this so many times. You come first, you always will, Mary and I are just dating. She has her own children—she doesn't need to be your mum. We're just having some fun. I think I'm allowed to see how it goes after everything and some time away might be the next step.'

'I don't want there to be a next step. Why does there have to be a next step?'

'Because I want there to be.' Dad looked exasperated.

I could feel white-hot rage in my chest. It was so inexplicable yet inevitable because I felt like I couldn't do anything about her and Dad. I just felt I had to put up with Mary whether I liked her or not. And I didn't like her. Not one bit.

Honestly, I'm not usually shouty like this, I promise! I'm a normal-ish thirteen-year-old (well, if normal means liking melted cheese on top of peanut butter and raspberry jam toast with tomatoes, then I am. Go on—try it! It sounds like it might make you yak, but it doesn't. It's like culinary Heaven).

'Mary just wants to be friends with you, that's all, Daisy. All this silent treatment and negativity must wear you out. You might find you get on if you just stop being so cross all the time.'

Uh-oh, the red mist took over. 'I don't want to be friends, ever! I hate her! She's vile and annoying and boring and I wish you'd never met her!'

'That's an awful thing to say!' He was shouting now and I hated it when he shouted because it usually made me cry. 'Mary is one of the nicest people you could meet. You have no right to say those things!' I just stared at him; somewhere buried deep inside of me I knew I was being nasty. I'd never ever said I hated her before. But I couldn't explain it. Seeing Dad with Mary made me feel—argh! I don't even have a word for it.

'Apologize now.'

I shook my head.

'Daisy, this is ridiculous. You can't say those things and expect me to just be OK with it. I'm not.'

I set my mouth in a firm straight line.

'Hate is a very strong word.'

Say sorry, say sorry, my inner voice said. But the

red mist singed my head and made my blood boil. I couldn't say sorry because I might say something even worse instead. So I thought it was better to stay quiet. Dad knew how I felt about Mary; how could he think I would be OK with a holiday?

Dad gave me a filthy look, turned his back on me, and stormed to the front door.

'I'll see you later; I'm going to work. This isn't the end of this conversation.'

I slumped over the table with my head in my hands. Why couldn't I just suck it up? I knew Mary wasn't a nasty person. I could see that, but it didn't make any of it OK with me. It was like I had no control over anything I felt. I could have done with someone to talk to and Izzy flashed up in my head. She had always been so good at calming me down about anything and listening. But we weren't friends any more. In Year Seven after Christmas we had exams and then we were all shuffled about in our classes. I wasn't with Izzy for any of my lessons—she was a total brain-box and in the top sets for everything. I found myself sat next to Celia in French, our year's queen bee. I never thought she would even talk to little old me. 'I love your bag,' she said unexpectedly one Monday.

'Oh, thanks. I made it.'

'No way, would you make me one? I love anything different like that.'

'Me too. I make clothes as well.'

'Wow, I wish I could sew. Did your mum teach you?'

'No. I taught myself. Mum was a fashion stylist though so I guess I get it all from her.'

'Wow, how cool. Is she still in fashion now? I want to be a model when I get older.'

'No, she's dead. She died when I was four.'

'Oh, gosh. Sorry!' Celia looked stuck for words so, as usual, when most people found out Mum was dead, I had to make it OK for them. Nana said this was fairly normal.

'It's fine, I'm OK.' I smiled. 'I think you'll make a great model.' She would as well—she was so pretty it was hard to look directly at her.

'Thanks. I'd like wearing all the outfits! What clothes do you make . . .?' We did no work in that French lesson, but we gradually became friends, sitting together in a lot of our classes after that.

When I made her bag, everyone else wanted one too, so I was run off my feet sewing, and Celia helped me by cutting the material into the right shape. 'It's my fault you have all these orders. The whole school wants a Daisy Hillman bag now!'

But Izzy didn't like her and I had no idea why. At

first I thought she was just jealous because we hardly saw each other at school now, but it was more than that.

Izzy looked pained when I eventually asked. 'She asked to copy my Physics homework before we were streamed and I wouldn't let her. No biggie, but she's super unfriendly to me now. Haven't you noticed?'

'No. Do you think you're exaggerating a bit? Because she's always really nice to me.'

'Of course she's nice to you. She's made you popular with your famous bags.'

'What's that supposed to mean?'

'Nothing, I'm just saying what I see. You're one of them now.'

'No I'm not!' She shrugged. She wasn't being mean but she was being weird. 'Look, I like her, OK? Is that a crime?'

'Nope, not if you want to get sucked in to the vortex of the Sirens. Good luck with that.'

Izzy called Celia and her gang the Sirens because they reminded her of the Greek mythological creatures that were half-woman half-bird that lured sailors to their death on the rocks of their treacherous island. See, I told you she was clever! They were intimidating in that popular girl clique way, but I'd never seen any of the crimes acted out that Izzy was obsessed over.

'They fake-like people as a laugh, to make them think they're friends, then diss them. Flaking. Soooo mean.'

'Is that what Celia did to you?'

'No. I don't want to talk about it. Just believe me when I say, she's not who you think she is.' I let it go and distanced myself from Celia out of allegiance to Izzy. She would never tell me what Celia said or did and I always wondered. I was pretty sure it was all a misunderstanding . . .

'Fart face, why you so quiet?' Celia asked one day after I sat somewhere else in Maths. 'Where you been hiding?' I shrugged and reluctantly smiled. 'You no likey me no more because I smell?' And she pulled a pig snout and made me giggle.

'Izzy said you asked to copy her homework once,' I casually said to Celia one day to get to the bottom of it.

'Who's Izzy?'

'The brainy girl I hang out with.'

'Oh, *her!* The one always reading a book?' I nodded. 'I would never copy homework. It's a one-way ticket to detention. Both of you get in trouble—I wouldn't want that!' And she smiled sweetly at me like butter wouldn't melt. Was Izzy lying then? Making it up about Celia being nasty? But that was the thing with Izzy—she hated lying and making up excuses (because she was rubbish at it) whereas I revelled in my ability to conjure up homework disaster stories worthy of a film trailer. Hmmm . . .

I was confused but knew talking to Izzy about it would get me nowhere—she had made up her mind about Celia; it didn't matter what I said about her being a real laugh. Over the year as Izzy spent more and more time with Ethan, a brainiac from her Maths set—I swear she was going to be a rocket scientist one day—I spent more time with Celia and by the end of Year Seven we were almost like total strangers. I found myself not knowing what to say to her and she irritated me with her obvious dislike of Celia (I never saw any evidence of Celia being mean to her). She invited me to her birthday party but it was the same day I was doing something with Celia, so I didn't go. I felt soooooo bad and knew I was being lame, but we'd drifted so far apart that I didn't know anyone going and it would have felt fake. I think not going to her party was the nail in the coffin of our friendship, however I didn't want to admit it. So beginning Year Eight, I felt like it was me and Celia, and Izzy and Ethan. But part of me worried, because Celia was someone I hadn't known since I was a baby, unlike Izzy. It's hard to let go of that much history and not panic . . .

Fast forward to today and I was sitting in the canteen at lunch with Celia and the gang. 'What's the matter with you?' Celia asked me. 'You've been in a grump since this morning.'

'I had a massive row with my dad.'

'Really, Daisy? Trouble on the home front? I'm no agony aunt, but you obviously need to talk about it, so come on, tell Aunty Celia all about it.' She patted her knee like she meant for me to sit on it. I laughed and shook my head and stayed where I was next to her.

'Well, yeah, you see, Dad wants me to go on holiday with his girlfriend and kids this summer.'

'That's great! Where're you going?'

'I don't know, that's not the point. I don't want to go.'

'Why?' She gazed over to Eva and Phoebe and glanced at the magazine they were furtively giggling about.

'Because I don't like Mary.'

'It's not fair, why can't we have boys that look like that at this school?' Celia butted in to the girls drooling. They laughed.

'Sorry, you were saying . . .' She turned back to me and batted her eyelashes all attentively.

'That I don't like my dad's girlfriend.'

'Is she a total cow?'

'No . . . It's just . . .'

'Then just go on the holiday. It's a holiday! Everyone loves a holiday. And when they're not looking, sneak off and leave them with the rugrats, and go and find someone else to hang out with . . .' I had told Celia so many times the kids weren't tiny, but she never remembered.

I sighed and looked out over the sea of heads and spotted Izzy two tables across laughing with Ethan and their gang about something. She glanced up and caught my eye. I must have looked worried or upset or something because she was about to dart her eyes away when she furrowed her brow and mouthed the words 'Are you OK?' across the room. I nodded and smiled weakly. 'You sure?' she asked.

'Yes,' I mouthed back. She nodded and looked away. In that instant I wanted to go over to her and tell her everything because I knew she would say the right thing and help me get out of the mess I had got myself into. But I couldn't. That wasn't in the rules. You switch allegiance and going back is always hard—I've never ever seen anyone do it. In fact I think it is impossible. I glanced at Celia giggling about the hot boys in the trashy mag and smiled. At least we had fun, she made me laugh till I wet myself and we did loads of cool things. That was enough, wasn't it?

Chapter two
Trapped

Dad texted me later that day when I left school to tell me Julia was going to pop in on her way home from work—there was a work emergency and he would have to stay late. I was secretly glad because I actually didn't want to see Dad right now. I still didn't know what to say about the whole Mary fiasco.

Julia had been Mum's best friend and was also Izzy's mum. I sighed—sending her in was like the whole Good Cop, Bad Cop scenario, with her obviously being Good Cop. She was probably under orders to try and gently force me into going on holiday.

'Hello!' Julia called as she opened the door.

'Hi.' I couldn't even smile even though I always loved seeing Julia, and I hadn't seen her much recently.

'Oh, you look like you need a cup of tea,' she said as she walked in.

'Yes, please.' Tea always made things better. As Julia

busied herself, I rummaged around for some chocolate biscuits in the tin on the dresser.

'So, how have you been? I can't remember the last time I saw you.'

'Not great. Dad wants me to go on holiday with him and Mary and her kids.'

'It might be OK,' Julia tried in an over-bright voice.

'I don't like her. We had a huge row about it.'

'I know, your dad mentioned it. He hates it when you two fight.' I instantly felt guilty. 'Why don't you like Mary, apart from the fact you think she's going to steal your dad and ruin your life?' Julia arched her eyebrows at me. I had never actually said that to anyone, but I guess I had made it obvious.

'Listen, I totally understand, it's hard to share your dad after all these years, but he deserves some happiness. Mary is a lovely person and very kind, and she loves your dad very much.' (Yuk, yuk, yuk!)

I just sat there in stony silence as she handed me my tea.

'So, how are you getting on at school? I hear the sewing is still going strong.'

'Yes, school's good. I'm making all sorts of stuff for people these days. Tablet cases are popular.' Julia smiled and looked sad.

'I think it's such a shame that you and Izzy don't see each other any more.' I always felt a little twist in my gut when she mentioned this.

'Sorry,' I mumbled. I felt like I was letting her down.

'No, don't be silly; I need to get over it! Izzy would kill me if she knew I'd even breathed a word to you about it. It's just that finding a really good friend—like your mum and me were—is very rare. All sorts of things then hinge on it.' I smiled this time. I loved the story of how Mum and Julia became friends; it always gave me a warm glow inside, even on a bad day like today.

Julia sat opposite at the table, reaching over for a chocolate biscuit at the same time. I dunked my one in my tea.

'Tell me again how you and Mum met.'

'Oh, you don't want to hear that story again! You must be bored to death of it by now!'

'Please! After the day I've had, I just want to hear something happy.'

'I never liked your mum at first. She hung out with the cool gang, but when we had the foreign exchange, we were thrown together because the two girls staying with us wanted to organize Sir Walter Raleigh's first ever prom.' She paused and took a sip of tea. 'Well, we worked so hard and spent so much time together, that when it came to the day of the prom we really let our hair down and bonded properly. Your Uncle Jonny was star of the show – his band were amazing. It was his rendition of "Summer of 69" that really cemented mine and your mum's friendship, dancing in the hall, having organized such a great prom together . . . We both couldn't believe we hadn't been friends sooner.' It was always weird when she mentioned Mum's big brother, Uncle Jonny. The last time I saw him must have been just after Mum's funeral, but I barely remember him apart from he looked a bit bedraggled and overweight.

'And then, years later, your mum dragged me to one of her work dos. I didn't want to go but she forced me, saying she needed some female support. We ended up in some dodgy club in town with a massive entourage and that's where we met Dave and your dad. Dave was the photographer Annie was working with, and your dad was some random guy who happened to be in the club with his mates. If your mum hadn't forced me to come out that night, I would never have met Dave, married him and had Izzy, and your mum might never have met your dad and had you!'

'Wow,' I breathed. 'So really, if you and Mum had never been friends and gone out on that night, Izzy and I might not be here today.'

'Bingo. As I said, such old friendships have lots of things hinging on them. You have a huge shared history all entwined together. I'm forever grateful for those exchange students making us help with the school prom, because they really made all this happen.' She smiled and I felt kind of flat. Izzy and I didn't have that any more . . . 'And every year after that until we left school, your mum and I organized the summer prom. And now you and Izzy go to the very same school, and get to enjoy the prom that we started all those years ago.' She went really quiet and looked a bit misty-eyed.

'Are you OK?' I asked.

'Yes,' she sniffed. 'I forget sometimes how much I miss your mum. She felt like the other half of me.' She wiped her eyes and laughed. 'Look at me, getting all emotional. Sorry!'

'It's OK, I wish she was here every day,' I said. I meant it. If she were here then Dad and I wouldn't be having this stupid row.

'I know you do, love. We all do. But I want you to know you're not on your own. If you want to talk about anything, you know you can ring me any time, or come to the house. It's such a shame we see less of each other now you and Izzy don't hang out.' And she looked dangerously close to blubbing again.

My eyes started to smart, and my throat throbbed with unreleased tears. I wasn't going to cry!

'And don't be cross with your dad. He loves you more than anything. He just needs to have a bit of fun after what he's been through. Now, do you want me to make you any dinner?'

After I'd pushed my pasta round my plate a few times, Julia took it off me.

'You look exhausted, love. Why don't you pop up to bed? Your dad's going to be a while yet. I said I'd stay until he got back.' I nodded and got up to give Julia a kiss goodnight. She hugged me close. 'It will all be OK. Just you see.'

In the hall on the way to the stairs a picture caught my eye. It was the photo of Dad and I on holiday in Spain a few years ago. We were laughing because he had just squelched vanilla ice cream on my nose and then took a selfie. Nana called the wall of photos a Rogues' Gallery, a jokey reference to criminals' mugshots that apparently hang up in a police station! There were lots of pictures of Mum, and there were quite a few of Izzy and I up there too . . .

Lying in bed it was impossible to sleep. The row kept flaring up in my head every two minutes—if only I hadn't said those awful things about Mary. I pressed

17

Pooh on my chest to try and calm me down. He was my snuggle rag and had been Mum's from when she was a baby. He was pretty much unrecognizable now – all traces of yellow fur whittled away over the years. No stuffing, just an ear, half a head, his belly and one leg. But I would never get rid of him, even though thirteen was way too old to still need him. I sat up and switched on the bedside lamp and the first thing I saw was the picture of Mum and me in a frame. Mum looked so cool and trendy with her white-blonde hair, cut into a really short asymmetric style. She was laughing and I was looking up at her sat on her knee. I was about three. I loved that photo.

I picked up the frame and placed it on my lap. 'I wish I could talk to you, Mum,' I whispered. 'I feel like I've messed everything up. I can't talk to Celia, and Izzy and I aren't really friends any more, but she's the one who would know what to do. I don't know what to say to Dad. I don't want to go on holiday with Mary, but it all came out wrong. I don't want to have a stepmum . . .' A tear squeezed out of my eye and plopped onto the glass, right on my face. I wiped it off, but another one fell in its place. How was I going to dig myself out of this?

Chapter three
You Spin Me Round

It was wet PE, but I wasn't there. I was daydreaming. When I'd got up this morning, Dad was already out at work, but he'd left a note.

Daisy,
I hope you managed to get some sleep. Julia said you were
very tired. I'd like to chat properly this evening. Hope you
have a good day. I've got pizzas for tea.
Dad x

I still didn't know what to say and my head was still in a real muddle. I wanted to see Dad now. It was ages until teatime. I just wanted to sort this all out, though I couldn't see how I was going to feel OK about Mary, ever.

'Daisy Hillman and you, Izzy Johnson, go and get the mats out of the cupboard. It's circuits, people!' Mrs Upton called out to us as we trouped through the gym door. I jumped out of my skin because I was miles away. Everyone groaned. I hated circuits. Then I realized I was teamed with Izzy and did my own internal moan. I hadn't properly talked to her for ages. I looked at Izzy and she was biting her lip. This was going to be awkward.

Izzy headed towards the cupboard and I followed behind her. She opened the door and peered inside. 'It's really dark.'

'Then try the light,' I suggested impatiently, then felt bad because I remembered Izzy had always been scared of the dark.

'I just flicked the switch. The bulb must have blown.'

'Bum. Come on then, let's get this over with.'

'Look, the mats are there under those medicine balls.' We both picked our way through the other PE stuff on our path to the mats. As my eyes grew accustomed to the dark, I could see the back of the cupboard. There were desks piled high and chairs too, along with string bags of footballs and netballs. And next to them were brown cardboard boxes with dates written on in permanent black marker.

'Ooh, look at those,' I said pointing to the boxes. 'I wonder what they are. I've never seen them in here before.'

'We haven't got time to find out. Come on, help me lift these balls out of the way.'

As Izzy struggled with one of the medicine balls I checked out the dates on the sides of all the boxes. I scanned them for any interesting ones. There were lots of Noughties and Nineties, then halfway down I spotted 1984-85.

'Izzy, help me move these boxes would you?'

'Why? We have to get these mats out. I can hardly lift this medicine ball. Help would be good.'

'Because there's a box in the middle labelled 1984-85, one of the years our mums were at this school. There might be something in here.'

Izzy made a huffing sound. 'Fine, but let's hurry up.'

'Go on then, open it!' Izzy said in an agitated voice as we finally freed it from the pile. 'I'm not doing time for this if we get caught.'

I ripped the loose tape off the top of the box, freeing the flaps.

'Well, if that's not breaking and entering I don't know what is,' she muttered. 'What's inside?'

'This!' And I pulled out a plastic bag. I held it towards the shaft of light by the door and could just make out the black lettering. It said *Ye Olde Curiosity Shoppe* in that corny ancient italic script.

'Quick, look inside. We're going to get caught soon.'

I chucked the bag at Izzy. 'You look; I'm going to see what else is in here.' But there wasn't anything apart from a few boring box files and some old books.

'Oooh, wow!' Izzy held a tiara in front of her face. 'Look, it's glowing!'

'Is it battery-powered?' I asked inspecting it.

'I don't think so, it was just like this when I took it out of the bag.'

'It's beautiful,' I cooed. It really was spectacular. There were hundreds of tiny white jewels encrusted all over the delicate design and they were sparkling in what limited amount of light there was available. It made the rest of the darkness feel even more saturated if that was at all possible. I was pretty sure the jewels weren't real. They couldn't be, surely.

'It's mesmerizing,' Izzy uttered. 'Look how it's getting brighter. How can that be happening?' I shrugged. I couldn't understand how something with no power was producing so much light. I touched it gently and it warmed my fingers. It was almost like it was buzzing but I couldn't hear it, just feel it.

'There's something else here.' Izzy rooted around in the bag and pulled out two pieces of paper. She held them next to the tiara so we could read them. 'This must

be the receipt for the tiara,' she said squinting at it then
dropping it back in the bag.

'And this is the prom flyer,' I pointed out. 'Look at
the king and queen's hideous outfits.'

'And their hair! It's massive! I wonder who drew the
picture? It's really good, so lifelike.'

'Give it here, please. I want to look closer.' I brought
the flyer up to my face and turned it round. 'Oh, there's
a voting form. Look!'

'Yes. And have you seen what's at the bottom?' Izzy
asked in an excited voice.

'Wow!' I squeaked 'Designed by Annie West—that's
Mum!' I whipped it over to check out her handiwork
again, tracing the lines of the drawing with my index
finger, knowing Mum had drawn this herself. I wanted
to sneak it home with me.

'I wonder if this is the famous prom when they
became friends?' Izzy said. 'Can you remember what
year it was when they met?'

I shook my head.

'Here, let me try on the tiara before we go? I wonder
if Mum ever tried it on . . .' Izzy handed it to me. I
placed it gingerly on my head and as soon as I did, I
could feel pins and needles prickle my skull.

'It would be so fun to go back and see the prom how

it was, Eighties style. All that bad fashion and gigantic hair,' I sighed, scratching at my head where the tiara was doing something weird. It felt hot now. 'It would be very different to this year's.' But what I *really* wanted to say was I would love to go back and meet my mum.

'Wow! You look amazing. It just does something strange, like it's giving you a halo.' I couldn't see what she meant. 'Oh! It's shining even more now; it's kind of pulsing, like a heartbeat, and changing colours. It *must* have a battery pack somewhere.' I felt a stabbing pain in my head and I ripped it off, but it had stopped flashing. I felt a bit dizzy and my head was pounding. A memory from the past popped up—Izzy and I camping in the back garden, lighting up our faces in the dark with a torch and scaring each other. I remembered it being so much fun, like this . . .

'Just put this tiara on for me,' I begged Izzy. 'I want to see if it does it again.'

'OK. Oooh, it's boiling!' she cried. It instantly started flashing like a Belisha beacon when she tried it on.

'Yikes!' I squeaked.

'What is it?' Izzy jumped.

'White sparks just jetted from it like shooting stars.' I gasped, feeling slightly alarmed as the dizziness threatened to take me over. 'The batteries must have gone haywire!'

'Ouch!' Izzy cried. 'It's burning me. What if it explodes?!' And she dramatically tore it from her head, hurling it into the dark and grabbed my shoulder to steady herself. But the force of her doing so pushed me backwards and Izzy fell with me, her hand still on my shoulder. The room was spinning, like after you get off the waltzer at the fair. We landed with a muffled thud on some footballs.

'What just happened, Izzy? I think I'm going to vom.' The cupboard got even darker like someone had sucked out all the remaining light.

Suddenly the broken light bulb burst into life, momentarily blinding me.

'Argh, who did that?' I cried throwing my hands over my eyes, terrified I was going to hurl.

'Oi, what're you doing in here?' A man was standing in the doorway glaring at us. As my eyes started to recover I could make out he was wearing a blue boiler suit and little black-rimmed glasses. He looked vaguely familiar though I couldn't place him. But, more alarmingly, Izzy was slumped totally lifeless in a heap where we had just fallen . . .

Chapter Four
Road to Nowhere

'We're getting the mats for Mrs Upton for indoor PE,' I stammered, making an extremely lame attempt at stumbling towards him partially blinded. A stabbing pain had set up shop behind my eyes. Izzy was still slumped on the balls, unmoving.

'Mrs Upton? Never heard of her. I don't know why you're talking about indoor PE, it's boiling outside.' Then he spotted Izzy. 'What's the matter with her?'

'Mrs Upton's our PE teacher,' I said, like he should know what I was on about. 'Izzy just tripped, she's OK, aren't you, Izzy?' Izzy remained silent. 'Izzy? Don't die on me, Izzy!' I leaned over and prodded her until she made a groaning sound.

'She doesn't sound OK.'

'She is, honestly.' I gingerly bent down and hissed in her ear. 'You better get up right now. I feel sick too.' She lifted her head and looked at me. She was as white as a pint of milk. 'Something weird's gone on.'

'The room's spinning,' she whispered like she was in pain.

'It'll die down if you get up slowly.' I offered her my hand and she grabbed it like a drowning person. I had to take deep breaths. What was happening to us?

'You two must be from the exchange,' the young man said, scratching his head like he'd just realized something. 'I thought I didn't recognize you. You're supposed to be out on the netball courts right now!'

'But . . . who are you?' I asked, confused.

'Mr Wakely, the school caretaker.'

'No you're not! Mr Wakely's much older.'

He looked shocked. 'I can assure you I *am* Mr Wakely.'

I stood there like a total banana because nothing he was saying made any sense.

How could he be Mr Wakely? Mr Wakely had grey hair and a weather-beaten face. This Mr Wakely was really young with no wrinkles and dark brown hair.

'Come on, I'll show you to the netball courts.' Izzy was looking as baffled as I felt.

We stumbled after him down the side of an empty gym where the sun streamed in through the skylights. Where was everyone? They were there a minute ago, inside because of the hideous rain beating down on the fields outside.

Mr Wakely delivered us to the netball courts. 'Here you go. Mrs James over there is the PE teacher.'

'Thanks,' I mumbled, the stabbing pain lessening slightly. 'Come on, Izzy.'

'What's going on?' she whispered worriedly. 'Why did we fall over in the PE cupboard?'

'Maybe the tiara gave us electric shocks.'

'Ah, two stragglers. Did you get lost from the changing rooms?' the teacher who must have been Mrs James asked.

The girls in the netball bibs stared at us. They all had similar haircuts, like they were from a secret society powered by hairspray. Massive fringes set hard into a Frisbee-like sweeping solid fixture sloping down over one eye. The variation was either short sides with long mullet-style hair at the back, or short sides and a wedge at the back, or shaved and a wedge.

'More delightful exchangers . . .' one of them whispered unkindly under her breath.

'Girls, you are . . .?' Mrs James asked and waited for one of us to introduce ourselves to her. She caught my eye and raised her eyebrow.

'Daisy,' I replied. Izzy said her name too.

'Great. Now have you both played netball before?'

We nodded dumbly and she handed us bibs on opposite sides. The headache and dizziness had now eased off and I felt slightly more normal. It was a bit like waking up after a very long sleep.

Mrs James blew her whistle to start the match. The team I was on never passed me the ball so I kind of didn't try to join in. Izzy had her feet trodden on twice and one of the girls knocked into me on purpose. 'Oh sorry, didn't see you there.'

Who *was* she? Who were any of them? Just then Izzy went flying, tripping backwards over someone's foot and smacked her head really hard on the playground, bringing down the girl who had bumped into me, who just got up and dusted herself off.

'Izzy, are you OK?' I ran over to her and she kind of lay there looking like she was trying not to cry.

'That was quite a crack you got there. Are you all right?' Mrs James asked, not sounding that bothered.

'No, it really hurts,' Izzy choked out.

'Can I take her to the office to get an ice pack?' I asked.

Mrs James laughed. 'An ice pack? There might be some frozen peas in the staffroom fridge.'

'Can I take her?' I asked repeating the question.

Normally if anyone fell and hurt themselves there was a huge fuss, and an air ambulance would practically appear from nowhere to see if they were still breathing. Well, not quite, I may be exaggerating a tiny bit but you get the picture. No one batted an eyelid this time.

'Yes, yes, do you know where you're going?'

'Yep!' I pulled Izzy up from the ground, now completely freaked out.

Izzy groaned. 'My head. I feel dizzy again.'

I put my arm around her to keep her steady as we started to walk slowly towards the exit gate. I looked cautiously over my shoulder; the girls were looking at us like we were from another planet but it was them that felt alien to me.

'When did they redo the steps at the back entrance?' Izzy asked dazedly as we approached them.

'No idea. I'm not in the School Architecture Appreciation Society.'

'They look completely different,' she wittered on as we walked down them. 'They're not as big.' Maybe they weren't, but I wasn't really that bothered. Right now I felt we had to get to the office, like it was my happy place.

'We just need speak to Mrs Hills. She knows everything. Maybe she'll know where our class is.'

I powered through the double doors and headed towards the office hatch by the entrance.

'I'm sure the entrance doors are usually black,' Izzy said quizzically.

'Does it matter?' I asked, looking at them and beyond to the ornamental pond in the courtyard. Hmmm, the fountain had disappeared. 'Who cares if they're blue, black, whatever!' It was weird that the fountain was missing though . . .

'Oh My God!' Izzy squeaked as I strode over to the office sliding hatch.

'What?' I barked.

'Look at that.' She was pointing to a massive poster just down the corridor on the left. It was a giant graph showing how much money the school had raised for its annual charity that year. It read: GRAND TOTAL FOR 1985 at the top.

'1985?' I whispered shakily.

'That's why everything's wrong—we're in 1985.' Izzy had turned deathly white.

'We can't be, it must be a joke,' I rationalized.

'Look at the date and time above the office.' There was a clock hanging on the wall with the time and the date and year underneath. July fourth 1985. The spins returned with a vengeance, threatening to knock me off my feet.

'This can't be happening,' Izzy cried after I too confirmed I could see that everything said 1985. 'I think I'm going to faint.'

I took several deep breaths, the kind you take when you know you are about to face something bad, like telling your dad you just spilled orange juice all over his laptop or that you've burned a huge hole in the carpet with the straighteners. (Yes, I have done both.)

'How did this happen?' I asked Izzy who had her head between her knees and was moaning softly to herself.

She looked up at me and glared. 'This is entirely outside the realms of anything I know about.'

'But you're good at Maths and Physics. Art and textiles aren't going to help us here. Not unless I can knit us a time machine from that poster over there.'

Izzy remained silent for a moment and then spoke, slowly easing herself upright. 'We could've come through a wormhole, but they're so tiny that we wouldn't fit in it, so that rules that out.' She may as well have been talking Swahili for all the sense it made to me. 'We might be having a joint hallucination and are really passed out in the PE cupboard. Maybe all the equipment fell on our heads and knocked us out as we were talking about our mums at school.'

I pinched my arm. 'No, that really hurts, so it can't be a hallucination. Surely that would wake me up. And what about when you smacked your head?'

'Hmmm, I don't know! I'm clutching at straws.'

'Do you think it was the tiara?' I asked. 'It was flashing and being weird and we both felt hideous.'

'What? Like it's magic or something?'

'Maybe. I can't think of anything else.'

'But that's crazy. Magic!'

'Look where we are. *This* is crazy. Anything's possible.'

Izzy sighed. 'I just want to go home.'

'How?'

'Back to the PE cupboard and see?'

'See what? What are we looking for?'

'I don't know.' She sounded desperate. 'A secret door, hole in the floor, anything that looks like it might be a way back. Maybe the tiara is still there?'

'What if we go back to the PE cupboard and there's nothing there? No secret door, no magic way back, no tiara, what then?'

'I hadn't thought that far ahead.' Izzy's eyes were bulging out of her head like she was holding in a scream.

'We need a Plan B, somewhere to stay while we figure out our next move, *just in case . . .*'

'Oh no, I'm not staying here with you. I'm going home *now*.' Just as Izzy was about to take off, the office door opened and a lady with mega-permed hair and fishbowl glasses poked her head out.

'Ladies, you're supposed to be in lessons, not holding a mothers' meeting out here.'

'Leave this to me,' I hissed at Izzy under my breath. She narrowed her eyes angrily but kept quiet. I had an idea. It felt off-the-scale crazy and I wasn't sure I could pull it off. To be honest, once we went down this road, there was no going back . . .

'Hello there.' My voice cracked, and I had to force myself to finish what needed to be said. 'We're the exchange students Daisy Hillman and Izzy Johnson. We're actually lost. Someone took our clothes from the changing rooms when we were in PE and we can't find the girls we're supposed to be staying with.'

'Oh dear, what a mix up. Can you remember who you're staying with?'

'Yes, I'm with Annie West. Izzy is with Julia . . .?' Panicking, I couldn't remember Julia's surname before she was married. It began with C. I gave Izzy a Death Stare hoping she would play the game. Now my eyes were bulging, pulling the face of our old wordless code that usually meant help me right now, or stay quiet, or get me out of here. I just hoped she remembered how it worked. She did.

'Cunningham,' Izzy said glowering at me.

'But those girls have two American students staying with them.'

'Honestly, we know that's who we're staying with.' I looked at her and gave her my best lost puppy face. However, getting the words out was such an effort because my mouth suddenly resembled a parched riverbed and my tongue felt furry and too big. 'I was so looking forward to meeting Annie's family. We had written to each other beforehand.' I tried to swallow but ended up coughing. 'Sorry. She likes sewing just like me and her mum is a hairdresser and her dad works for the council. We each have brothers called Jonny, and both of them play guitars in bands—what a coincidence!' And what a massive fat lie—I don't even have a brother! Please, please say yes. Believe me, lady, I need to stay. She hesitated. I wasn't sure she was going to go with it . . .

'We've had so much paperwork to do with this I don't know whether I'm coming or going,' she said eventually. 'Let me see if I can move the other girls somewhere else. There was someone on a waiting list to be a host family after a last-minute drop out. Leave it with me.'

I was so happy that a tiny mouse-like squeak escaped from my lips and my face felt like it was going to split in two from grinning uncontrollably. She beckoned us into the office, presumably to make some calls. We waited by the door in silence. I kept digging my nails into my hands to see if I woke up. Izzy refused to look at me.

'All done!' Glasses Lady chimed after five minutes. 'You're all sorted.'

'Thanks! What shall we do now though?' I asked expectantly, my ears pounding with blood. Focus, Daisy!

'You could come with me to find them. I think they're doing athletics.'

'Great, we'd love to.' I almost wanted to hug her for not allowing Izzy the chance to escape. I was shaking and my palms were so wet I had to wipe them on my shorts. I bet my top lip was a sweatfest too!

'Follow me then.'

Izzy looked at me shocked; I shrugged in a What Can You Do kind of way. As we pushed through the double doors I half expected her to leg it to the gym but she didn't; she silently followed Glasses Lady to the left and out to the playing fields.

She led us to the edge of a grass track where people were running round. 'Wait here. I'll go and get them.'

'As usual, you haven't thought this through,' Izzy started as soon as we were out of earshot. 'What if meeting our mums in the Eighties makes the universe implode on itself? We might disappear into a black hole or something. Let's go back to the PE cupboard now— no one will see us. It's not too late.'

'No! There's no way I'm missing the chance to see Mum.'

'They'll know we're lying!'

'Why would they think we're lying? We knew our mums' names and if there's another family waiting in the wings then it's all sorted and no one will ever know.'

'We don't even know what exchange school we go to,' Izzy pointed out.

'Yes we do. How many times did your mum tell us? Must have been a million. It was the American School in Paris, remember?' Izzy chewed her lip and refused to answer.

I was about to meet my dead mum, the person I have loved in a picture for my entire life. But she wasn't a photo in a frame, she was real and she was going to be here any minute. As Glasses Lady approached, I could see two girls with her. One was short with a solid hairsprayed helmet of brown hair and some severely dodgy trainers that couldn't have been cool in any era.

The other was taller and striking with very short blonde hair in a sweeping impressive fringe . . . I felt the bottom fall out of my stomach and my palms instantly start to sweat all over again. I'd never felt so nervous in all my life. I thought I was ready for this. Now it was really happening, I wasn't sure I was. Mum . . .?

Chapter Five
Take On Me

'Annie, Julia, these are your exchangers for the next two weeks,' Glasses Lady said. 'There's been a bit of a mix-up.'

My legs were shaking. I couldn't look directly at Mum because I could feel my eyes start to well up and my throat throb with the effort of holding in tears. I was falling apart. So I closed my eyes to try and calm down and grabbed Izzy's hand.

'Hello,' Mum said. 'I'm Annie. Why weren't you in the meeting earlier?'

'I er, don't know. I didn't know there was a . . . er, meeting. We got lost,' Izzy eventually managed to stutter out. I opened my eyes and looked at Izzy. She was bright red and I could see her eye twitching like it always did when she was stressed.

'Oh, are you OK?' Mum asked me staring right into my eyes sparking something so deep down inside me, some hazy memory of her asking me that in another lifetime, that a violent tsunami of nausea suddenly overtook me and my ears felt muffled. I clutched Izzy's hand again, almost crushing her fingers.

'Keep it together, Daisy,' Izzy whispered. 'I know it's hard, but you have to try.'

My legs wanted to buckle but I stiffened them so they couldn't, bolstered up by Izzy's encouragement.

'You've gone very white,' Mum continued.

'I forgot to eat lunch,' I stammered nervously.

'I have a banana back in my bag,' Annie offered kindly. 'Do you want that later? It's a bit squashed.'

Tears automatically sprang from the corner of my eyes and I furiously blinked them away. I tried to smile and squeaked out a reply: 'Yes thanks, Mum.' Oh noooooooooo! Izzy flinched.

'Oh ha ha,' Mum said.

'Sorry!' I blustered, the tears disappearing immediately as panic mode set in. 'I don't think you're my mum—that would be ridiculous! That's not what I meant. I just said it because you were acting *like* my mum, you know, being nice with the banana. I mean, offering me the banana. I *love* bananas. They're my favourite fruit. I don't like brown ones, though I don't care; I'll eat your banana even if it's squished—Ow!' Izzy pinched me, stopping me mid-flow. *Nice with the banana*? What was I saying? I'd obviously had a severe attack of verbal diarrhoea.

Julia was looking at me like I was crazy and Mum was raising her eyebrows in a totally baffled manner.

'No worries. It's just a banana,' she said bemused.

I looked right at Mum. I *had* to think of her as Annie from now on; it was too strange to think of her as Mum. We were the same age for a start!

'Right, shall we get your cases?' Glasses Lady said.

'Er, we don't have any, er . . . cases,' I faltered, desperately trying to think how this could have occurred.

'Why? What happened to them?' Annie asked, disbelievingly, I thought. Could she tell we were faking?

'Because er . . . they just didn't arrive.' Think, Daisy! Think! 'They . . . got lost in transit,' I delivered with an anguished voice. 'We have no clothes or toothbrushes or anything. The teachers have no idea where they got lost.'

'Oh, you two girls really are doomed today, aren't you?' Glasses Lady piped up. 'Well, Julia, Annie, you're just going to have to share your clothes with the girls until their cases turn up.'

'How long will that be?' Julia spoke properly for the first time. 'I don't have much spare stuff.' Her face was burning bright red and she wouldn't look at us.

'I'm sure it won't be more than a few days,' Glasses Lady assured her. 'Have you got anything you need to pick up?' she asked us.

'Nothing. We just have these clothes we're wearing,' I said in a sad voice.

'We still need to get changed though, and get our bags and stuff,' Annie said as we walked towards the main school building.

'Well, why don't you two go off and do all that and I'll take these two to lost property and sort them out with some school uniform so at least they have something for school, and we'll meet you in the foyer?'

The girls walked off, separately. Julia striding ahead obviously keen to get a move on, Annie not making any effort to catch her up.

Lost property was in the office and Glasses Lady handed over two lots of uniform each. 'That should keep you going for a bit, and save you wearing the others' clothes at school.'

Glasses Lady got back to work and left us in the foyer to wait for the mums. It still hadn't sunk in that I was going to go back to Annie's house. My mum was alive. I was breathing the same air as her.

'This doesn't mean we're staying, just so you know.' Izzy rained on my parade as I dreamed about spending time with Annie, and telling her I was really her daughter . . .

'I *know* that.'

'Do you? This is your *mum*, Daisy. It's freaky enough for me, and I see my mum every day. You . . . don't.'

'I'll keep it together, I promise.'

'That's not what I'm worried about.' She looked round as if to make sure no one was listening. 'You can't tell your mum anything about the future. About her . . . dying. Or who you are. Nothing. Which is why we have to head straight back home tomorrow the first chance we get. It's obvious we've landed just before the crucial point when they become friends. We need to leave as soon as we can.'

'Why?'

'You know why! Because things have to stay the way they were before we came: the mums being best friends and meeting our dads because of your mum's job. If one thing messes up from that equation you and I won't exist.'

'But what if I did it in a way that didn't mess with anything?' Though right at that moment I had no idea how I would do that. Izzy had a point—it was very complicated.

'NO!' she yelled, so loud that a few kids out early from lessons turned to see where the noise was coming from. 'The safest thing to do is to not mention anything,' she whispered. 'It's bad enough that the Americans aren't staying with them tonight. You have no idea what one tiny insignificant change can do—it can ripple out into the universe and affect all sorts of things—it's called the Butterfly Effect. Once the school realize we never existed the Americans should be reunited with our mums after we leave tomorrow so we'll remain just a blip.'

'Keep your wig on. I promise I'll be cool. It'll all work out.'

'You better because our lives depend on it.'

'Shh, here's Mum . . . I mean, Annie,' I said, my heart leaping into my mouth. She was in her uniform now carrying some trendy neon-pink army type bag plastered with all sorts of cool badges and key rings, rammed with folders and books. You could tell she was a fashionista, even with bad Eighties hair.

'Where's Julia?' Izzy asked her.

'No idea. Her stuff was in a different part of the changing rooms. I just left when I was ready. You coming?' she asked me. Gosh, they really weren't pally at all. How on earth did they ever manage to like each other? The bell exploded right near my ear and I dropped my school uniform to cover my ears. Annie laughed.

'Can't we wait for Julia?' I asked when the bell stopped ringing.

'If you want...' I kept taking sneaky glances at Annie because, weirdly, I did keep forgetting she was my mum. She wasn't the shadowy figure I vaguely remember from being little—she was very much alive and looked like the girl I had pictures of back home. It felt like Dad was going to shake me awake any moment and tell me I was late for school.

I almost didn't notice Julia in the throng of kids spilling out of classes. She kind of blended in with the masses in a grey blur of conformist uniform. Even her school bag was grey, devoid of any embellishments. Outwardly, she and Annie were chalk and cheese.

'Come on then, let's go,' Annie said. 'Follow me.'

'Where do you live?' Annie asked Julia outside the gates.

'Right near you!' she said, sounding appalled. 'I walk past your house every day!'

'Well, I've never seen you!'

No one said anything and it was slightly prickly.

'Look, are we walking home?' I asked. 'Is it far?' I knew how far it was—Nana had lived in that house forever. But Annie didn't know I knew that.

'Yes, we can all go together then, can't we?' Annie

said and started walking in the direction of Nana's house with Julia trailing in her wake. Izzy pulled me back as I tried to catch up.

'One more thing,' Izzy whispered, 'I know this is going to be hideously hard for you, but just try not to give any information away when you get to Annie's house. We have to act like we're almost not here.'

'How am I going to pretend that? I'm not invisible! This is my mum, Izzy!'

She looked sad and nodded. 'I know, Daisy. It's huge. Mega, but just try and hang out with your mum without changing anything else.' She touched my arm gently and smiled. 'Remember, one tiny bit of information has the ability to alter things and not necessarily for the better. This is an emergency crash-landing until we escape tomorrow morning at school. OK?'

'Whatever, Miss Bossy Boots.'

'I'm just reminding you!' she replied huffily.

'Yeah, well don't. OK?' Izzy looked cross but didn't say anything else. She wasn't going to be at Annie's house. How would she know what I got up to? I didn't see what was wrong with having a proper chat. It was only going to be one night.

We all said our goodbyes at Annie's (or Nana's) garden gate. Izzy looked over her shoulder at me as she walked away. Her eye was twitching and she looked pretty scared. I felt a pang of apprehension; I suddenly wished she were staying with me too . . .

'I think Mum might be at home,' Annie said as she rummaged for her key in the army bag. 'She wanted to be here when you arrived. Mum? We're here!' Annie chucked her key in the pot on the table in the hall. She pushed open the kitchen door, the handle slamming into the wall. 'Oops.'

'You kids! I may as well knock the wall through. You're always trying to do it with the door!'

Nothing prepared me for the shock of seeing Nana thirty years younger, sitting at the kitchen table. Her hair wasn't short and grey—it was a dark brown shoulder-length bob with quite hideous white plastic hoop earrings poking out from underneath. Her line-free face had a splattering of freckles. I tried to work out how old she must be but couldn't do the maths. She looked happy to see me, making my nerves vanish.

'Hello, Daisy. The school rang and told me there'd been a mix-up.'

I wanted to rush and give her a big hug. She was Nana but Old School!

'Would you like a cup of tea? Do they have tea in Paris? Or do you all drink coffee and eat croissants?'

'Tea would be great, thanks.'

'Please sit down. Annie, find the biscuits, would you.' Just then I heard the front door go once more. I wondered if Grandpa had come home early from work to meet me. The kitchen door slammed into the wall, the handle banging into the well-worn groove already there from years of battering.

'Here he is, Prince Charming,' Annie said with a hint of sarcasm.

A boy sauntered in, the vision of cool itself. Dimples on show, blond hair all wavy and refreshingly hairspray-free, smiling like he was in a Gap advert. It couldn't be, could it . . .?

He made a theatrical bow like he was flapping a feathered cap in my direction and then burst out laughing.

'Don't listen to all the stories she tells you. They're not true!' His eyes were twinkling with the light of some mischief he'd yet to unleash. He was a charmer; so good-looking it was illegal, and had the best smile I had ever seen.

'This is my brother, Jonny, also known as Prince Charming.'

I choked on my tea, spraying it all over the table. Annie thumped me on the back. Wow, Uncle Jonny— whatever happened to you?

Chapter Six
Back in Time

'I've always loved your lasagne,' I murmured quietly after we'd finished dinner. Whoops! I'd blabbed again. Izzy would kill me if she were here.

'What did you say?' Annie asked sounding puzzled. 'Did you just say you've *always* liked Mum's lasagne, like you've had it before?'

'No.'

'You did, I swear I heard you say it under your breath.' She looked at me like I was a crazy person.

'Annie,' Nana said in a warning tone. 'I think you misheard her.'

'I didn't!'

'If she said she didn't say it, then she didn't say it,' Grandpa said quietly. 'Daisy is a guest in this house, remember.'

'I really didn't say it.' I tried to look as innocent as possible without resembling one of the real mugshots from a genuine Rogues Gallery at the cop shop. 'I just said how much I liked it. It's the best I've ever tasted.' And I flashed Nana a mega-trega-watt smile that I hoped would ingratiate me for eternity.

'Ooooh, you know how to say all the right things,' Nana gushed as she cleared away the plates. Annie looked at me strangely.

'So, Daisy, tell us about yourself,' Nana said. 'Do you speak French?'

'No!' I panicked; was I supposed to?

'It's the American School of Paris, Mum,' Annie explained, coming to my rescue. 'It's an English-speaking school for kids abroad if their parents are working in Paris away from home. Lots of American and British kids go there too, as well as French kids who want to be taught in English. We've learned all about it! But they're still taught French, I think, aren't you?'

'Oui!' I said and Nana laughed.

Acting invisible with my nosey family was going to be impossible.

'Go on,' Jonny laughed. 'Tell us your darkest secrets. We won't tell anyone!'

'Well, I don't have any brothers or sisters and I live with my dad.'

'Where's your mum?' Annie asked inquisitively—it felt like a verbal punch.

'She's dead.' The kitchen went silent. Even the kettle clicked off at that exact moment, making it feel like we were in an airless soundless box. I didn't mean it to be dramatic or even tell them, but it just popped out.

'Oh gosh, I'm so sorry, forget I asked. I feel terrible,' Annie wittered, looking flustered. 'You must think I'm awful for poking my nose in.'

'Don't be silly. I don't think you're awful at all. It's funny because it's like Mum was still here only yesterday and no time's passed at all. It feels like I could still bump right into her . . .'

Annie blinked and turned bright red. 'Now I feel worse.'

'Annie, she died when I was four; she was in a car accident on the way back from work.'

'Oh phew, I thought she'd died recently or something,' she blustered, then went even redder. 'Not that it makes it any better. Oh, sorry—I'm saying all the wrong things.'

'Maybe stop talking?' Jonny said smiling sadly. 'Sorry about your mum by the way.'

'Can we pretend that I never said any of those things and start again?' She smiled sympathetically at me, making my gut twist into a knot.

'Sure,' I squeaked out, wishing that we could pretend

she'd never died and that we could start again as a family, just her, Dad, and me.

'Oh, Daisy,' Nana sympathized, 'that's a traumatic thing for you to go through.' She looked so pained that I had to swallow hard so no more tears made an appearance today. It was sad—it was more than sad—it was a crime and here I was with a chance to be with Mum again . . . should I tell her the truth?

Annie gave me a spare toothbrush at bedtime. I was going to sleep in my PE T-shirt. 'Do you need anything else?' she asked as she hovered by the bathroom door.

'No. I think I'm OK, thanks.'

'Good, well, my room's just there if you need anything.' She stepped in to the bathroom and I thought she was going to give me a hug goodnight. So I did what anyone else would do faced with their long-lost previously dead teenage mother: I gave her one first. Errr, big mistake. HUGE.

'Ewwww, what are you doing?' she screeched, visibly recoiling as if I'd dog-licked her face.

'Errrr, saying goodnight?' I stuttered. 'What are *you* doing?'

'Getting my hairspray off the side of the sink.' D'oh. She looked horrified. I'd committed the mortal sin of a too early PDA. We'd only just met, but really we hadn't . . .

'I was just saying goodnight how we say it in Paris, you know, the double kiss and a hug?' I tried to recover the situation gracefully. Though I was about as graceful as an elephant on Barbie's ice skates.

'Oh, right. Well, I don't, er, think I'm, er, ready for that yet,' she stammered, grabbed the hairspray and darted backwards out of the door. 'Night!'

Great, we'd really got off to a fab start . . .

'So, you promise we can leave straight after assembly?' Izzy whispered to me in the hall on Friday as Mr Jimpson the headmaster droned on about dull school stuff. 'We can't risk getting stuck in the Eighties over the weekend.'

'Yes,' I hissed unhappily. I didn't want to go home. I wanted to get to know Annie, but I knew Izzy was right about messing with time. If we left now, things would stay the same. We would still exist—that was something I didn't want to mess with. I wanted to make sure I saw Dad again. If only we had more time here . . .

'How was it at Julia's?' I whispered so no one apart from Izzy could hear.

'Weird. She's very quiet and doesn't seem to have many friends. I tried to find out who they were but she wasn't keen to chat.'

'Maybe she's shy?'

Izzy nodded. 'How was your evening?'

I was just about to tell her when Mr Jimpson ramped up the volume.

'As I was saying, unless we get some volunteers to help organize the end of year summer disco, it will be cancelled. It's up to you, people! There's a final call meeting at morning break in the library. No one turned up to the one last week, so I have no option but to cancel the event, if there are still no shows for volunteers.'

In the dark recesses of my brain Mr Jimpson's words kick-started something. He was talking about the prom, but it wasn't the prom—it was the summer disco. Our mums had yet to turn it into a prom . . .

As we filed out of assembly I dragged Izzy to one side behind an art display, avoiding the mums.

'Hey, you do realize the school disco Jimpson was talking about was the school prom Annie and Julia have to organize—it's how they become best friends.'

'Yes, I know. That's why we have to leave straight away—we don't want to stop that from still happening.'

'But don't you see—it's already too late. We've changed everything anyway. The Americans were in that assembly somewhere, *without* our mums, ready to claim the prom with their new hosts. What if they don't want to go back to our mums after we've left? What then?' Izzy looked like she wanted to run.

'I don't know,' she finally admitted.

'I also have a mega gut feeling that the tiara is behind this mess,' I continued. 'I think it transported us here, to 1985.'

Izzy took a deep breath. 'So what we need to do is . . . stay?' she admitted very slowly like it hurt.

'Yes, and help organize the prom, and make sure the mums become friends.'

'Then what?'

'Escape after the prom using the tiara—I know it sounds ridiculous, but this *is* ridiculous!' Izzy looked as if she was having an internal battle with herself.

'We need to find it then.'

'So let's go and look now. I bet it's still in the PE cupboard.'

'The Americans will be at the meeting later,' Izzy puffed as we ran. Luckily no one was in the gym as we pushed through the door.

'Don't worry, I'll come up with a plan in lessons.'

We picked our way over to the back of the cupboard. It was totally different to yesterday when we had to get the mats. There were no boxes, no desks rammed at the back, just net bags of footballs and PE paraphernalia.

Izzy darted over the mats to where she'd dropped the tiara yesterday. I searched further round the other side.

'It's not here,' she said worriedly after we'd pulled the cupboard apart. I sat down with my head in my hands. Think, Daisy, think. 'Maybe it isn't the tiara,' Izzy offered up. 'Maybe a time portal will open up after we've made the mums become best friends. So we have to make sure we're here on time when it opens up again.'

'Maybe,' I said, not convinced. I was so sure the tiara would be here. So many thoughts were whizzing round my head about the tiara, Mum, the prom takeover plan that I couldn't think. 'Look, let's go to lessons before we get in trouble—we don't really want to draw attention to ourselves. We'll say we got lost.'

At break we found ourselves loitering outside the library at the top of the stairs, having run all the way there to beat the crowds. There had been no time for explanations. The mums had no idea where we were.

'What do they look like?' Izzy asked quietly. We hadn't bumped into either of the Americans yet.

'I don't know. Your mum did show us pictures once. Anyway, they'll have accents.' As we stood there twiddling our thumbs, I realized that I must have spent more time with Izzy in the last not-quite-twenty-four hours than I had done for at least a year.

'I can hear them!' Izzy hissed as American accents floated up the stairs.

'Oh, hi! Is this where the disco meeting is?'

'The meeting's actually been cancelled. Er, the headmaster has decided to let us have a disco, but only if the teachers organize it this year instead.' I smiled innocently at them.

'Oh bummer. How come?'

'One of the teachers volunteered with a few other staff to take over the whole thing. I think they have some ideas they want to try out.'

'Why're you guys standing here then?' one of them probed distrustfully. I was glad we were in school uniforms—it made us less suspicious-looking.

'They asked us to be here just in case anyone turned up so we could let them know.'

'Oh, OK. Such a shame, we had so many awesome plans for it. Perhaps we could help out?' D'oh—do-gooders!

'Yes, that would be a great idea,' I smarmed. 'Why don't you give me your names and I'll . . . er . . . pass them on to the teachers involved. I'm sure they'll find you if they need any help.'

The girls wrote their names down on pieces of paper they had in their bags: Lindy Craven and Tracy Ross.

They sounded like proper cheerleader names. Give me an L, Give me an I . . .

'Well, thanks, girls. See you later!' Lindy drawled, flicking her solid fringe. They waved as they trotted back down the stairs, hair bouncing as they went.

'Now for the next part of the plan . . .' I clapped my hands together eagerly.

'This better work,' Izzy nervously added. 'Or we could both be toast . . .'

CHAPTER SEVEN
Everybody Wants to Rule the World

'Are we too late for the disco meeting?' Izzy asked timidly, approaching the desk at the back of the library. I could tell the teacher was gutted we'd turned up. Her face fell faster than a bungee jumper in a suit of armour.

'No, no, I'm still here, aren't I?' She sat back down and sighed as if we'd just told her wine was illegal. She pulled her pad and pen out of her bag.

'So, I'm Miss Avery. What are your names and why do you want to help with the school disco?' She gestured for us to sit down too.

'Izzy and Daisy,' Izzy trotted out. 'We feel the school needs something *more* than a disco.' It was like she was reading the news. All she needed was a weather report and she would have nailed it. I was impressed. She normally hated lying or tricking people.

The teacher smirked and then pulled a straight face. 'But you girls aren't even at this school. You're on the exchange, right?' We nodded. 'So what makes you think you know what this school needs? And what exactly is "more than a disco"?'

'A prom!' I cried. 'You should do a prom!'

'*A prom*? Like they have in America? How on earth would we do that? This is just a school disco. A prom is like a ball, isn't it?'

'We have them at our school every year. I've organized them before. I know how to do it,' I said, lying.

'But there are only two of you. Unless there are more of you, I can't see how you would get this done.'

'What if we come up with a plan, with drawings and ideas and get them to you by the end of the day? It could make money for the school too.'

'Yes, but you need to find at least two more volunteers between you or it can't go ahead.' She looked like that's what she wanted as well.

'We have two girls who would help, Annie West and Julia Cunningham. They're the girls we're staying with.' I was absolutely certain I could see Miss Avery's face jerk like she wanted to scream at us.

'OK, if you manage to get me some plans to the staffroom by the end of today and can guarantee two extra girls, I will put it to Mr Jimpson and see what he says.' Izzy grinned at me triumphantly.

'What now?' she asked me as we loitered in the shade

behind the bike sheds five minutes later. 'I'm finding it so hard to talk to Julia, I'm not sure I'll ever convince her to help at all.'

'Why?' I asked puzzled. I had a million things I wanted to talk to my mum about, which would be tricky without looking like the stalker she probably already thought I was. 'Just drop the prom into conversation—at the right moment!'

'I keep freezing up every time I want to ask or say anything. Don't you feel freaked out that you're here with your mum? But she's our age. I mean, that just blows my mind. They have no idea they're going to have us, get married, be proper grown-ups.' Izzy looked a bit het up. 'I know stuff about her that she has *no* idea about!'

'Yes, I get what you mean, but I've wanted to see my mum again since forever. This is a dream come true for me . . .'

'I know it is, but I just feel weirded out. Julia isn't what I expected. She's so quiet—she would prefer to read a book than do anything. And she's always scribbling in her little notebook. I don't know what to say to her. So I hid in the loo last night just to be safe in case I gave anything away—though the chances of that happening were very slim. She probably thinks I'm a proper nutjob.'

'Bad period excuse?' She nodded—failsafe skive method every time.

'You're going to have to make more of an effort—bond with her.'

'How? About what? It all feels so fake. She's as quiet as a mouse.'

'Well, make her glad you're here. We have to get her on board—our lives depend on it.'

Izzy looked pained. 'What is it?' I asked her, trying not to get irritated.

'Nothing,' she said heavily, in that loaded way when it was anything but nothing.

'Just say it.'

'All I keep seeing when I look at her is Mum, back in the future. And we're not really getting on at all . . . at the moment.'

'Why not?' This was news to me.

'She just doesn't get me. Has no idea what anything's like now. She's always saying when she was a girl blah, blah, blah and interfering, telling me what to do and getting cross for no reason—but what does she know? Stuff going on for me isn't the same as it was for her. Anyway, how can she remember—it was all such a long time ago.'

'Oh that's a shame.' I'd always thought Izzy and Julia

got on so well, something I'd always fiercely wished I could share with Mum. But really, I had no idea what had been going on with Izzy for the last year . . .

'Sorry, I know you don't have a mum and this must seem ungrateful . . .'

'Then you're going to have to see her as a thirteen-year-old girl and not your mum; someone you have loads in common with. Try that?'

'And maybe you should do the same?' Izzy replied looking right into my eyes, unnerving me. 'Forget Annie is your mum, and just get through this the best we can.' I pursed my lips.

'Fine.' I just said that to please Izzy and stop her worrying. As far as I was concerned, Annie *was* my mum, and I wanted it to stay that way . . .

'Hey, girls, this is Dawn, she's coming back to mine for tea.' Annie and Julia were waiting by the school front gate as the rest of the stragglers left for the evening. Julia was reading a massive chunky book and didn't look up. We'd just handed in the plans for the prom.

'Hi,' Dawn said breezily. I recognized her from netball. She was the one who Izzy had brought down when she fell over. She had the typical brown mega-solid sprayed hair and a very pretty, fox-like face. And before she even spoke I felt like I didn't quite trust her. Gut instinct maybe . . .

'Haven't you got hairspray in Paris?' she said innocently to Izzy on the walk home, who had long brown hair that she barely dragged a brush through. 'Top tip—no one really does ordinary hair over here.' She made it sound like she was giving kindly advice to a hopeless hairstyle victim, when in fact she was sticking the knife in. I waited to see what Izzy would do.

'I'm allergic to it,' Izzy said, smiling sweetly. 'It turns my hair into a bird's nest.' Oooh, Izzy! I wanted to clap, but chuckled to myself instead. Dawn just gave her a sickly smile. Yep, we weren't here to make friends with *her*.

Once we got to Annie's gate, Izzy looked at me and gave me a mega-trega Death Stare and thrust something into my hand without the others seeing.

'Bye, have a great weekend!' Annie called to Julia and Izzy as they traipsed off.

'Jeez, those two will have about as much fun as a vegetarian at a butchers,' Dawn quipped looking for easy laughs after they'd gone. 'They barely made a peep all the way home.'

'Dawn—don't jump to conclusions; you've no idea what they're like,' Annie replied, smiling.

'We'll see. Old Nose-in-a-Book will probably drag your mate round a library all weekend. Anyway, where's Jonny? Is he back from school yet?' she said all eager. Uh-oh, so she fancied Uncle Jonny? Interesting!

'No, he's got band practice tonight.'

Dawn visibly popped like a balloon. I felt incensed that she was muscling in on my precious time with Annie but knew I couldn't get rid of her and was going to have to join in if I wanted to hang out. I had wanted to see if Annie knew anything about baking. I always remembered Julia, Izzy, and me making cakes years ago. Maybe Annie and me could make something after Dawn left? The girls headed for the kitchen so I nipped to the loo and unscrewed Izzy's note.

Meet me in Annie's front garden at 11pm tonight. I will wait by the gate.

Izzy

The total lack of phones or email was bizarre, making writing secret notes the new form of communication. It was something Izzy and I hadn't done for years, since before we had phones anyway. We were always sneaking notes under the desk, making each other giggle in class.

'So, have you heard the news—Sharon Day got tickets to Live Aid. Did you know Wham! are playing? And Duran Duran. I don't know who I like more.' We were sat at the kitchen table after eating dinner.

'Oh, Wham!, definitely,' Annie replied eagerly. 'Who do you like?' she asked me kindly, trying to draw me into the conversation.

'Er, Wham!?' I said hesitantly, not sure who they really were.

Dawn ignored me. 'Yes, you're a Wham! girl for sure, Annie.'

I zoned out; Dawn was rabbiting on and on but none of it was reaching my brain. I just stared at Annie and sipped my cup of tea, wishing Dawn would go so we could make cakes or something.

'Oi, whatsyourname again?' I was shocked out of my reverie by Dawn's name-calling.

'Daisy!' I said hotly; I really didn't like her.

'Daisy,' Dawn said in her sweetest voice but she

wasn't fooling me, 'what bands apart from Wham! do you like then? You've not said anything for ages.'

Oh no, caught out on the hot spot. Annie looked expectantly at me. I had no idea about Eighties bands. I didn't want to let her down by being uncool.

'Er, all of them?'

'That's a cop out! Just say one.' This felt like a test.

I racked my brains to try and think of just one band that I might know. Bingo!

'Oh, I know. ABBA!' I practically shouted, so pleased that I had some sort of answer. They were Eighties, weren't they?

'What?' Dawn cried, as if I had just said I liked drowning defenceless kittens as a hobby.

Annie suppressed a giggle and lowered her eyes as I desperately checked her out to see if I had failed. I had.

'No one likes ABBA!' Dawn explained to me like I had just beamed down from Mars and was going to have LOSER tattooed on my forehead forever.

'Well, I do!' I said, realizing I had to look convincing, try and claw back some credibility. 'They're big in Paris. Everyone likes them!' Why hadn't I said that other band, Duran thingie?

'Really? Paris is well behind the times then!' Dawn

laughed. There was a bit of an awkward silence so I broke it.

'Look, I'm going to go to bed. My tummy hurts.'

'Oh no,' Annie said sympathetically, 'what's up?'

'You know, the usual monthly *thing*.'

'Oh, right, poor you. That's rubbish. Do you need anything?'

'That would be great, thanks.'

Annie took me upstairs and found me some pads in the bathroom cabinet.

'Here you go, I hope you feel better in the morning.' And she patted my arm. I remembered having to tell Dad a few months ago when I first got my period. (Cue Dad going puce, 'Ah, yes, have you got tummy pains? Er . . . do you feel sick?'—like *he* knew!) Thinking of Dad made me worry. I hoped we weren't listed as abducted or anything scary like that. I hoped it was like that film *Back to the Future* and no one was missing us because our time was frozen.

At eleven, I sneaked downstairs and out the back door to the side gate. Izzy was already there.

'Come on, let's go for a walk round the block,' she said quietly. 'We don't want anyone to hear.'

'So?' I asked when we stopped near the edge of the park and sat on a bench under a streetlight.

'We have to have a plan. The exchange ends the day

after the prom—that's two weeks to organize an escape *and* the prom.' Sitting in gloomy silence, neither of us voiced our concerns about *how* we would get home . . .

'Do you really think it was the tiara?' Izzy asked eventually. 'It was glowing and everything and we felt so wrong. Do you think it's the answer?'

'Yes I do, but you said something about a portal?'

'No, I've been thinking about that. The school would be overrun with cave people and knights from the Crusades popping through a gap in the time space continuum—it would be happening all the time. It has to be the tiara.'

I nodded, not understanding a word she'd said but it sounded plausible all the same.

'But the tiara is stuck back in the future,' Izzy pointed out.

'Oh bum, you're right.' We sat in more silence, me wanting to punch my own head to bang out some brilliant idea.

'Hang on, hang on!' Izzy suddenly yelped. 'The tiara *is* here somewhere.'

'No it's not, it's in the future.'

'But think—where did it come from in the first place?'

'Ye Olde Curiosity Shoppe, it said so on the bag.' I rolled my eyes, and then had a light bulb moment. 'Duuur, oh yes, it's in 1985!'

'The girls must have bought it from that shop for the prom.'

'Which proves we need to be in charge of the prom so we can have the petty cash to buy the tiara and see if it works!' I said triumphantly.

'Yes yes, you're sooo clever . . .' And she pulled out a pad and pen from her bag. 'So let's make a few notes. The main points are . . .' and she started scribbling away with me peering over her shoulder.

Operation Hairspray

1. Force mums to help with the prom

2. Sweet-talk Jimpson that we can ace the prom

3. Mums MUST become BFFs

4. Find the tiara—our ticket home

5. Sneak out the back door of the prom like ninjas

'Operation Hairspray?' I queried.

'Yes!' Izzy cried. 'Every secret plan has to have a code name.'

'Roger that!' I laughed. 'I like it. A good solid name like everyone's Eighties hair.'

'Exactly!'

'We can start hunting for the tiara first thing tomorrow,' I suggested.

'OK, we could both search on the . . . hmmm, where do we look?' Izzy looked stumped.

'The *Yellow Pages*? I guess they have them in 1985. No Internet here!'

'Yes, we'll look in there. The shop must be local, and then we'll go and buy it once we have the petty cash.'

'But we can't leave until we're sure the mums are friends, so that means staying until the prom, and nipping off with the tiara once everything's worked out—dead easy!'

We perched on the bench all planned up and nowhere to go.

'We still got it,' Izzy said quietly.

'What do you mean?' I asked.

'Oh.' She looked embarrassed. 'You know, we still know how to do stuff, make things work. Like we . . . er, used to.'

I sighed—she was right. I tried to imagine being trapped here with Celia and I drew a blank.

'Look, I'm really tired. I'm going.' Izzy got up abruptly and began to walk away, back to Julia's house. I suddenly felt awkward, watching her retreating back.

'Hey, Izzy?' She turned round. 'You're right, we do still have it.'

I could just about make out the grin on her face through the dark.

CHAPTER EIGHT
Holding Out for a Hero

I was dreaming about being sung to by Mum when I was sick with a cold or something. I had a vague memory of her putting a damp flannel on my head and singing me the 'Sleeping Bunnies' song while I lay in bed. She was stroking my head. It felt so nice. I wanted to stay there forever.

'Wake up, wake up, Daisy . . .'

'Mum?'

'No, Daisy—it's me, Annie! Are you feeling better?' The pure happiness created by the dream just briefly slipped from my heart, making me panic, but realizing Annie was there reinstated it instantly.

'Eh?' Oh yes, my bad period! 'Yes, thanks. What time is it?' I rubbed my eyes, just to make sure it was her and not another dream.

'It's ten. I thought I would come and wake you. Mum's made pancakes and you might want to come down before Jonny eats yours.'

'OK, give me a mo.' I was going to have to get her in Team Prom today. I pulled on some trackie bottoms that Annie had lent me and followed her to the kitchen.

'Here she is, sleeping beauty!' Jonny crowed from the kitchen table. 'Oooh, what hedge did you get dragged through?' He winked at me and made me laugh. I liked him. He was a few years older than us; he must have been fifteen or sixteen. I have only one sketchy memory of him after Mum's funeral and he looked pretty dishevelled. There were also rumours flying around that he'd gone off the rails and distanced himself from the rest of the family. Maybe Mum's death was the last straw.

'Have you eaten all my pancakes?' I asked cheekily.

'Would I do that?'

'Yes!'

'They're in the oven,' Nana said. 'I had to hide them from him or he would have inhaled the lot. Here . . .' She placed a hot plate next to me, with squeezy lemon and a bowl of sugar.

'Thank you!' I LOVE pancakes.

I finished breakfast and sat there looking at Annie flicking through *Jackie* magazine.

'Annie, have you got any clothes I can borrow?'

'Yes, sorry, let's go upstairs.' I hadn't actually been in Annie's room properly since we'd arrived. I had obviously been in it in the future—it was where I stayed when I was at Nana's overnight. It was very red and white stripes, very er . . . Eighties *un*cool! Then I spotted something on the bed that took my breath away. Pooh! But he was whole, if a little bashed. He looked like he'd had his ear stitched back on. I picked him up and sniffed him.

'Awww, embarrassing. That's Pooh!' Annie giggled nervously. 'I've had him since I was a baby.'

'I know.' Anne looked at me funny then I realized. D'oh! 'I mean I can tell you have—he's a bit battered up. I have one too like this—it was my mum's.' She smiled and I placed him back on the bed.

'So we're going shopping with Dawn today.' I felt my stomach drop. Really? Dawn? Urgh! 'Then I thought we could go and get ice cream on the river. Mum and Dad want to take us out for dinner later so said they'd meet us at the ice cream parlour.' Annie looked so pleased with her girlie plan that I couldn't say anything. The disappointment was crushing.

'That sounds great, but I don't have anything to wear.'

'We can rectify that!' Annie opened the flimsy white wardrobe and rustled around, pulling out some jeans, shorts and a blue-and-white stripy miniskirt, and various tops.

'Here, try these. I don't really wear them.'

'Thanks so much. Do you have a pair of shoes?' She dived back in and pulled out a pair of strappy sandals that weren't too hideous. 'Great. I really appreciate this.' I turned round to go back to my room and try them on when I spotted the sewing machine. It was on the other side of the room perched on a little desk.

'Ooooh, I love your sewing machine,' I cooed. 'What do you make?'

'Everything! I made that stripy miniskirt I gave you to try on.' I held it up, dropping the other things on the floor. It was nicely made and finished off properly with folded over seams—all neat and tidy.

'It's really good.'

'Thanks. Do you sew?'

'Yes, all the time. I make lots of stuff, I started off making bags though and ended up selling them at school.'

'Look what I'm making now,' Annie said and stooped down and reached under the sewing desk for a floppy straw bag full of material. She pulled out a bright blue batwing T-shirt. 'I want to sew sequins all round the collar,' she said. 'What do you think?' If anyone else had made it I would have cringed—it was so Eighties! But Annie had made it . . .

76

'I love it! Maybe we could do some sewing today? Have you got any spare material? Maybe I could make a T-shirt too?'

'What about shopping with Dawn?'

I would rather eat a whole packet of dry cream crackers smothered in anchovy paste, I thought privately, but smiled at Annie. 'Can we go shopping another day? Tomorrow?' And that would give me time to possibly 'be ill'.

'Shops don't open on Sundays!' Annie looked like I was mad. 'Anyway, I think Mum wanted to show you some sights tomorrow!'

'Oh.'

'But if you'd really rather do sewing?' I nodded. She looked super pleased and grinned. 'I would actually, too! I'll ring Dawn and tell her. She hates it. It'll be nice to have a sewing buddy for a change.' I crossed my fingers, hoping that Dawn would rather eat dry cream crackers and anchovy paste than come over here to sew.

Bingo! Cream crackers it was!

'Did you pattern-cut your bags properly?' Annie asked, setting up the sewing machine.

'Kind of. I followed tutorials on, erm . . . videos, like a sewing class sort of thing. I had a book too,' I stumbled. 'I just make it up half the time.'

'Do you want me to show you properly? I taught myself from this book, look——' and she reached into her sewing bag and pulled out one of the books Dad had said was Mum's most treasured possession. She'd got it for her eleventh birthday and when I was born had written in it:

Dear Daisy,
I hope this gives you as much help and joy as it has given me over the years.
All my love
Mummy xx

Annie handed her book to me but I wasn't ready. I dropped it, bashing the spine.

'Oh no! I'm so sorry!' I gasped, hands shaking, picking it up trying to uncrumple the dent. 'I feel terrible.' I'd damaged the book that she'd kept in such good condition.

'Don't worry, it's fine. It's just a book.'

'My mum had the same book. I have it at home.' I opened it up to the place where she would one day sign it and ran my fingers across the blank space where her note was going to be, not sure what I was going to say next.

'Oh.' I looked up at Annie and met her gaze. 'I'm sorry.' It was the perfect moment to blurt out everything. But fear stopped me—I wasn't prepared, didn't know what to say, or how to say it. And worse of all, what if I messed it all up and then had to endure the rest of the time trapped here, with Annie being scared I was a crazy person who might kidnap her in her sleep? In the split second it took for that scenario to flicker across my brain, I pulled myself together. This needed careful planning and perhaps in a few days' time would be better.

'Go on then, I'd love you to show me proper pattern-cutting!'

I'd spent years wondering what it was like to have a mum just *being there* doing normal stuff and here I was finally experiencing it! I sneaked furtive glances at her as she busied herself drawing out a pattern for me—I was hanging out with my mum, just like any normal person! It finally felt like a missing piece of the jigsaw from my life had just slotted into place. I never wanted that piece to go missing again . . .

The words Operation Hairspray suddenly muscled their way into my head, reminding me I needed to nail point one on Izzy's list . . .

1. Force mums to help with the prom

'Look, there's something I need to tell you,' I began.

'Oooh, what? Gossip?' Annie looked very eager.

'No! I put us and Izzy and Julia forward to organize a prom instead of the lame school disco.'

'You did what?' Annie's eyes widened like saucers.

'I thought it would be a brilliant idea. They are so much fun at our school; everyone gets so excited about it.'

'No one goes to that rubbish school disco. No one would turn up! I don't want to help a disaster in the making.'

'Not even if we have to make amazing costumes for the king and queen, and have a band, and hot dogs and crowning ceremony, time off lessons . . .?!'

'No! You're both crazy if you think that'll work.'

Her words stung—she had no faith in me. I felt pathetically like I was going to cry and had to stick my fingernails into my palms to stop the tears from falling. I needed to rescue the situation and change her opinion of me and the prom fast.

'Look, whatever you might believe, the prom is actually all part of a plan to skive off lessons while having some fun.'

Annie looked up from her drawing and I took that as encouragement to plough on. Something I'd said to Izzy flashed into my head: *Forget she's your mum and just think of her as a thirteen-year-old girl.*

'Look, imagine if we pull off this prom. It could be the most spectacular event this school has ever seen. Especially if we can get Jonny's band to play.' Annie just stared at me. 'If we organized it, all the credit would go to us, well, you, and you would have bonus points here for the rest of your life. You could do anything and get away with it. You'd be famous . . .' I paused dramatically. Please, please, please say yes.

'Look, it's so not my thing . . .'

'But think of the glory!' and I spread my arms wide. 'Everyone in school would see your costumes. Mr and Miss Popular could wear them!'

Annie narrowed her eyes. The silence was excruciating.

'How much time off lessons do you reckon?'

I could have kissed her, but knew that was probably a step too far!

'What's going on?' I hissed to Izzy as we reached the school gates and we lost the mums in the chaos.

'I asked Mum, I mean Julia, if she would help, lied to her that Annie was, and that we might get time off lessons, but she wouldn't budge,' Izzy said in a pained manner. 'We spent all weekend going round Richmond Park, having picnics and visiting Hampton Court. She's very booky, completely different to Annie. How on earth were they ever friends?'

I shook my head. 'I've no idea, but she has to come to the meeting today.'

At the end of registration, Mr Creasy, our form tutor, asked all four of us to come to the front of the class.

'Now, I have just been given your names on a slip of paper. You all have to go to Mr Jimpson's office immediately after assembly. What have you been up to?'

'What's going on?' Julia asked jumpily as we approached the double doors to the foyer near Jimpson's office. 'Why are we going to the office, and why aren't any of you worried?'

Time to action the next objective on the Operation Hairspray, even though we'd only half accomplished number one!

2. Sweet-talk Jimpson that we can
   ace the prom

'It's about the prom,' Annie said. 'You know, the fact that we might be organizing it.'

'But I said no,' Julia cried.

'Too late, we're almost there,' I said. 'Come on, it'll be so much fun. We can't do it without you.'

'You'll have to. I'm not coming.' And she stopped dead.

'Look, you have to come to the meeting because Mr Jimpson has asked you to,' Annie said matter of factly. 'If you don't come you might get in trouble. You can always tell him once you're there that you don't want to do it. OK?'

Julia looked furious, but nodded her head.

'Ah, ladies, please sit,' Mr Jimpson indicated the awaiting chairs once we were in his office. We all shuffled into place with Miss Avery behind us. Mr Jimpson was a really tall man with a ruddy complexion and glasses. He must have been older than Dad. I found him intimidating. I bet when he shouted people's hair puffed up like in a cartoon.

'So, I've looked through these plans. Very good ideas there. Who came up with these?'

'Me, sir,' I said shakily.

'And you're on the exchange? What's your name?'

'Daisy, sir.'

'And you're Izzy,' he nodded towards Izzy.

'Yes.'

'Well, I like this idea a lot. And as you say, it could make money for the school—we're always looking for ways to do that.' He stretched his arms out behind him on his chair.

'How do you think you'll get pupils to buy tickets? You need to sell a lot. What's your hook?'

The others looked at me to speak. Erk!

'Well, I think Jonny West's band is going to be the major draw—he is very popular at school. Also, the nomination process for king and queen of the prom. By having an open vote, starting when you announce the prom, kids will want to get involved.'

'And Jonathon's band have agreed?'

I nodded enthusiastically, praying Jonny would play or we were toast. I crossed my fingers behind my back.

'OK because I can't see it working without the band.' I knew that! 'Also, what do you mean an open vote?' he asked interested.

'Well, in order to get the three choices for either the king or queen, there has to be an initial vote across the entire school. You can vote for anyone you like via the polling station in the office. The top three names with the most votes will be the candidates for king and queen.

'Great stuff!' He clapped his hands together. 'So, ladies, this is an awful lot of work for you—are you sure you're up to it? You might need extra help and some time off lessons. Miss Avery here can assist in any way she can. The office ladies will sort the tickets and posters for you. Those designs need to be handed in by tomorrow first thing. Who will be doing that?'

'Annie? Would you do it?' I asked her. She nodded enthusiastically.

'That just leaves it to me to mention it tomorrow in assembly, drum up business. You girls report directly to Miss Avery for the petty cash and all other concerns, OK?' We all nodded. 'Anyone got anything else to add?' I looked nervously at Julia, She didn't say a peep.

Point One and Point Two had been fully achieved.

1. Force mums to help with the prom ✓

2. Sweet-talk Jimpson that we can
ace the prom ✓

'Right, off to lessons. Well done!'

As soon as we were a good distance away from his office, Annie let out a whistle.

'I've never ever seen Jimpson so upbeat. He's so into this!' She sounded genuinely surprised and excited. 'Thanks, Julia, for sticking with us.'

Julia smiled for the first time since I'd met her.

'That's OK. I guess I'm part of Team Prom now,' she said gruffly, her cheeks flushing.

'Yes, you are,' Annie laughed. 'We need you!'

'So, we *have* to get Jonny's band now . . . We should have asked him before the meeting,' Izzy said wringing her hands. 'Annie, what do you think? Will he do it?'

'There's only one way to find out. Ask.'

Chapter Nine
The Wild Boys

'So, Annie, I hear you're helping with the school disco,' Dawn drawled mockingly in the lunch queue. 'I can't believe you'd want to get involved with *that*.'

I can't believe you're not having a knuckle sandwich for lunch.

'Hey, it'll be great fun. You should come and help— we need extra hands, don't we girls?'

All three of us looked panicked. Don't say yes. Don't say yes . . .

'You kidding me? No one will want to come to *that*. It's for the first years.' Phew.

'Thanks for your support, Dawn,' Annie said sounding let down. 'Well, we're still doing it. You don't have to come, do you?' Dawn looked massively put out. Good, I thought. Julia and Annie need to start bonding, fast. I wanted to stick a rocket up Julia's bum to get things going.

'So, shall we agree that Annie and I will start off making

the costumes?' I began. Everyone nodded. 'Annie's handing in the ticket and poster designs tomorrow.'

'And Julia can plan the stage with me,' Izzy continued, smiling at Julia who actually looked pleased with her job. 'Then Annie and Daisy can join in alongside making the costumes, but we will all help each other at the same time when we have to.'

'First we need Annie to bag Jonny's band,' I said, 'or none of this is going to get off the ground!'

'Jonny's band?' Dawn almost spat out her baked beans everywhere. 'What happened to Mr Sheppard on the wheels of steel?'

'There is no Mr Sheppard, Dawn. This is a prom—we need a proper band,' Annie said telling her straight.

'Well you can ask him now,' Dawn crowed. 'See what he says about playing at your disco. He's just walked in.' Maybe it was me but she seemed certain he would say no.

Annie stood up and waved in an insane manner, obviously trying to embarrass him. It worked. He pulled an 'I am too cool' face and gestured for her to calm down. Then he came over.

'What, Small?' he said. 'Did you have to act like a total wombat in the lunch hall?'

'What's up, Jonny? Scared all your admirers will laugh at your little sister?'

88

'Yes, I have a rep to protect,' and he shuffled up his collar and acted all retro like someone from the film *Grease*. Annie rolled her eyes and laughed.

'How would you feel about playing at the school end of year prom with your band, next Friday?' she said all at once very quickly so the words stumbled into one another. I sat with my fingers crossed under the table.

'Wow! What prom? I never knew about this,' he looked around at us all. 'Hang on,' he said starting to chuckle to himself. 'Do you mean the school disco where Mr Sheppard tortures everyone with his bad taste in music?'

'No, it's a proper prom, like in America, with a band and hot dogs and a prom king and queen. I'm helping to organize it with these girls. It's going to be the biggest thing this school has ever seen!'

Jonny burst out laughing. 'Is it now?'

'Yes! We just need a band, and you're the best.'

'Oh yeah? Flattery will get you everywhere. Tell me more . . .'

'Jimpson won't let us do it without you!' Annie looked anxious.

He darted his eyes towards each of us in turn—we all gave him pleading looks. His dimples really were showstoppers. If he were going to play, the prom would surely be a sell-out.

'Is this true?'

'Yes. Mr Jimpson has given it the OK on the condition your band plays,' I replied, butterflies zipping around my belly. He had to say yes. 'He's allowed us a budget and everything.' He bit his lip and had a think.

'Right, I'm not promising anything, but let me talk to the guys and I'll let you know later.' And he smiled all round.

'Wow, thanks, Jonny!' And Annie jumped up and hugged him.

'Gerroff! Bye, girls . . .' And he slunk off to go and be cool somewhere else.

'Do you think they will say yes?' Dawn asked obviously surprised.

'I think they will,' Julia said quietly. 'Jonny looks like he wants to do it and he's the lead singer, isn't he?'

'Yes, but that doesn't mean it's up to him,' Dawn scathed like Julia was stupid, making her recoil. 'They might all say no.'

'Well, let's hope they don't!' Annie said, smiling at Julia and pulling a face at Dawn.

Fast forward to after school and someone barged into our group at the gate.

'Jonny!' I cried. I saw him before anyone else. Dawn suddenly transformed her usual smacked-bum face to wide-eyed fluttery lashes of a Disney princess. Oh, *really*?

'Hello, Jonny.' She batted her eyes at him. I did a silent fake retch into my mouth and Izzy hit me. She was stifling a giggle; so was Julia who rolled her eyes at Izzy.

He just looked at her and said a very brief, 'Hi.'

'Any news?' Annie asked hopefully.

'Maybe,' he said winking and falling into step with us as we made it out onto the street.

'Come on, Jonny, put us out of our misery,' I pleaded. I could see Dawn out of the corner of my eye practically push Izzy out of the way in order to get nearer.

'The guys all said yes they would do it.' All of us cheered. 'But, you're going to have to let me see the set design because we all need to fit around what you have planned, so I'll have to come to a meeting or two?'

'Well, that's easy because we'll just hold them at home,' Annie said. 'Thanks, Jonny. That's so amazing.'

'Yeah, thanks,' I added.

'What if nobody turns up?' Dawn asked clearly surprised Jonny had lowered his standards.

'Why wouldn't they turn up?' Izzy asked her.

'Because no one ever does.'

'This time they will,' Julia said bravely, obviously bolstered up by Jonny joining Team Prom.

'What makes *you* so sure?'

Julia went chilli red but Annie smiled at her encouragingly.

'Because these girls have got great plans. People will want to come.'

'Yeah, Dawn! If we're playing EVERYONE always turns up!' Jonny swaggered, blowing Dawn out of the water.

Dawn looked like she'd swallowed a whole lemon, pips and all. Hope you choke, I thought.

That night we sat cosily at the kitchen table, Annie beavering away on her designs for the ticket and poster, me sketching costume ideas.

'Could you pass me the . . .' I asked Annie realizing I needed the rubber, but she was already handing it to me.

'How did you know?' I gasped.

'Telepathy!' Annie laughed and winked.

Time to implement the next point on Operation Hairspray:

3. Mums MUST become BFFs

'Annie, what do you think about having a sleepover?'

It wasn't every day that you got to have a sleepover

with your thirteen-year-old mum! I mean, who wouldn't want to force their mum to do truth and dare? Or maybe not! Ha ha.

Annie looked up distractedly from her drawing. 'What? A sleepover?'

'Yes, where we all hang out here, sleep in your room, eat sweets, chat, mess around, play games, and make stuff for the prom.'

'Oh, right, yeah. That sounds like an American slumber party in those *Sweet Valley High* books.' I nodded having no idea what books she was on about.

'So, you keen?'

'Yes, let's do it. Today's Monday, sooo we could do it this Friday, if you want?'

The sleepover was the perfect opportunity to get Annie and Julia to bond. I mentally patted myself on the back for practically ticking off the next item on the list. This wasn't going to be so hard . . .

On Tuesday, when Izzy and Julia called for us on the way to school, Izzy dragged me off with her to walk in front, leaving Julia and Annie behind to 'get on'.

'I need to talk to you. I looked up Ye Olde Curiosity Shoppe in the *Yellow Pages* last night. It doesn't exist. Julia had never heard of it either.'

'So what are we going to do?'

'I don't know. We have to have that tiara though, I'm now mega sure of it.'

We scuffed our shoes along in silence, not really knowing what to say next. Not *daring* to say it.

'So, unless we can find it, we can't get back . . .' I said eventually.

'Correct,' Izzy replied gloomily. 'And we have no idea which one of the girls found it last time.'

'But they found it before, so we could find it again.' I ignored the frantic little flutterings in my tummy. 'We just need to keep trying—we'll look properly when we go shopping for the costumes.' I needed that tiara; it was as simple as that. Because I had to warn Mum about the accident so she would be there when I got back . . . .

'So, I have some good news,' Mr Jimpson announced in assembly. 'You lucky people are going to be treated to a prom next Friday, instead of the usual school disco.' Cue heated whispering travelling round the hall like a Mexican wave. 'Shhh! Yes, next Friday, you can vote for your Prom King and Queen, dance to the music of the Wild Boys—' whistles of appreciation from the crowd, '—and generally experience Sir Walter Raleigh's first ever prom!' Someone started cheering from the back of the hall, where the older kids sat and others joined in—it felt like a football match.

'Tickets go on sale this Thursday at the office and in the canteen,' he continued above the noise. 'You can also post your prom king and queen nominations in the office at lunchtimes starting tomorrow. The nominees will be announced next Wednesday. This prom needs you people, so get involved!'

'Wow,' Annie hissed sounding astonished. 'Nothing like this has ever happened before. People seem genuinely excited.'

'No pressure then,' Julia said making a face. 'We really have to pull this prom out of the bag. Everyone's expecting it to be amazing.'

I looked over at Dawn who had a strange smile on her face. I had a dreaded feeling that it meant trouble for us.

It turned out I was right.

Chapter ten
If You Love Someone, Set Them Free

'So, if the theme is going to be Flower Power because it's summer,' I said in the meeting on the field at lunchtime, 'I think we should decorate the stage with flowers.'

'But that'll be really expensive,' Julia insisted. 'Maybe we could make giant flowers and trees from cardboard. Real flowers are lovely, but they're also very small and no one will see them.' Julia fiddled with the button on her grey cardie and looked down at the grass.

'I think that's a great idea,' Annie agreed enthusiastically.

'I can come up with some designs this evening and then we can start making them this week. Nothing complicated,' Julia suggested, smiling. 'Here, I've got some ideas in my notebook already. I carry it everywhere with me.' And she took out a small navy blue hard-backed drawing book filled with sketches for the prom and other stuff—people's faces, trees, buildings, animals—everyday stuff.

'I never knew you were *this* arty,' Annie said in an admiring tone. 'You always seem so into books and English.' Oh oh, they were properly talking and Getting On!

'I love making things too,' Julia replied shyly.

We were getting tantalizingly close to ticking off number three on Operation Hairspray when a whirlwind hit. Dawn.

'Hi there, ladies, room for me?'

'Hey, Dawn, what you up to?' Annie asked, shifting sideways so she could squeeze into the circle.

'Well, I thought I'd come and help, you know, join Team Prom. You did ask me.'

But you said NO! I wanted to scream at her. You only want to join in now because it looks like it might be popular. And because Jonny's playing . . .

'Oh, great!' Annie cried, sounding pleased. 'We need help all right.'

'What do you want me to do?' she asked flashing us all fake smiles.

Julia sighed and quietly closed her notebook and slipped it into her school bag.

'Well, Julia's going to design the stage set tonight and then we can start painting and making it all in art and at lunchtimes.' Dawn nodded like she really wanted to help. 'And Daisy and I are making the costumes.'

'What about stage stuff? Setting up on the day—will Jonny be helping us out?' I caught Izzy's eye and we both rolled them at the same time. How could Annie not see what was going on?

'I hope so. I have no idea where all his stuff goes,' Annie laughed obviously oblivious. 'Oh yes, Daisy thought we should have a prom sleepover on Friday, you know, bring stuff to make and do for the prom, eat sweets, stay up late, that sort of thing. You should come too.'

No, no, no, no, no!!! I looked at Izzy and she widened her eyes and then gave me a mega Death Stare. I glanced over at Julia, she seemed to have crawled back into her shell, just when her and Annie seemed to be getting on. Grrr . . .

The rest of the week flew by in a blur of gluing, painting, skiving off the exchange stuff because we weren't on any lists (yay!); charity shop foraging for all the costumes and material; and hunting all over town for Ye Olde Curiosity Shoppe (it still eluded us— ARGH!!!!).

'Listen, Dawn, why don't you man the voting boxes instead of us all taking turns?' Annie patiently suggested on Thursday lunchtime after another botched attempt at helping. 'We'll just carry on with the prep until prom.'

'Well, if you're sure . . .' She looked at us gleefully.

Friday rolled swiftly around and on the way back from school Dawn asked: 'Will Jonny be in when we get home?' As if I needed any more proof of her interest in the prom.

'Do you think she knows she's got a flashing neon sign strapped to her head saying "*I Fancy Jonny*"?' Izzy whispered.

'It must be weighing her head down—her neck's going to snap any second!'

Julia must have been listening because she laughed and then hurriedly turned it into a cough as Dawn turned round and stared suspiciously.

'Aren't you a bit freaked about having a sleepover with our *mum*s?' Izzy asked in a hushed tone as we approached the house.

'Why? It'll be fun.'

'It'll be weird. I don't want to know about boys Mum might fancy or her innermost secrets. Mega cringe!'

'Well, stick your hands over your ears at that point! Who gets this chance to know their mums properly before they became mums? I want to know EVERYTHING!' Izzy laughed at my enthusiasm. 'They might be just like us.'

'I can't see how Julia is like me at all. I love sleepovers. I practically had to force her to come.'

'Yeah, I noticed she doesn't talk much. Maybe she's the silent moody type?'

'I dunno. I think she's very shy, which is so odd. Mum, shy?'

I laughed. Yes, the Julia I knew couldn't be accused of being shy.

'Look at me, I'm the prom queen!' Dawn brayed later as she pranced around the kitchen in the shabby dress we'd bought from a charity shop.

'Yes, Dawn, you'd make a fabulous prom queen,' Annie joked rolling her eyes. 'Now stand still while I cut the skirt off.' Annie and I had planned the outfits—the queen would have an elasticated-waist skirt and sash that would fit anyone and the king would have this ridiculous ruffled shirt that was so big it didn't matter, and a cape. Obviously everything would be covered in sequins!

'We need a tiara or a crown,' Julia said timidly. 'I might have one from when I was younger, dressing up and stuff. I think it used to be my mum's.'

'Oooh, yes please. Maybe we could look for it tomorrow when we go home?' Izzy suggested hastily. Maybe the tiara never came from a shop. Maybe the name on the bag was sending us on a wild goose chase?

'I have an idea. Why don't you go and look for it *now*?' Dawn said looking directly at Julia. 'Then we can see what it will look like with the outfit.'

'No, I think we should look tomorrow,' Izzy replied firmly. 'Julia will miss bits of the sleepover otherwise.'

'Well, it would be better if she went now,' Dawn insisted in a cheery voice. 'Why wait till tomorrow? She's not going to miss anything! What do you think, Annie?'

'Oh yes, that would be great,' Annie said absently, concentrating on cutting the skirt off the dress, her brain obviously not engaged. 'If you don't mind. Then we can tick it off our to-do list.'

Julia just nodded and Dawn flashed a sneaky triumphant smile.

'Then we should come too, Daisy?' Izzy gave me a Death Stare. I nodded balefully.

We walked in silence; I felt like something was going to happen but I wasn't sure what. When we got back to the house Julia just stomped straight upstairs.

'Are you going to look for the tiara?' I called after her.

She didn't say anything.

'Is she OK?' I asked Izzy.

'I don't know.'

'She's just so different to your mum in the future. I wonder what happened to change her.'

'Daisy—she's only thirteen! How can she be anything like Mum now?'

I shrugged. I didn't really know what my mum was like as my mum. I only knew what I saw now aged thirteen.

'I think I'd better check what Julia's doing,' Izzy said gloomily.

'I'll come with you.' So we trudged up the stairs, the TV blaring from the front room, disguising our presence to Julia's parents.

Izzy pushed open the bedroom door and Julia was lying on the bed staring at the ceiling. Her room was very girlie with a yellow theme and a giant round wicker chair covered in teddies of all sizes—different to Annie's with her hideous Eighties bold stripes. A white bookcase faced the bed bursting with books, all the spines battered and creased like they had been read a million times.

'You OK?' Izzy asked uneasily. Julia shrugged, keeping her gaze upwards. 'Aren't you looking for the tiara?' She shook her head.

'What's going on?' I asked. 'Was there ever a tiara?'

She remained silent; then just as I was about to

ask it again, she spoke hoarsely. 'Yes, Mum has one somewhere.'

'Shall we look for it?' Izzy suggested carefully. 'You know, so we can see what it looks like?'

'You can if you like. I'm not coming back to the sleepover.'

'How would I know where to look?' Izzy looked worriedly at me. 'We really want you to come back.'

She sat up and looked right at us. Her eyes were a bit watery like she was fighting back tears. 'I don't want to.'

'Look, is it because of Dawn?' I asked. 'I don't like her either, but she's Annie's friend and she's helping with the prom.'

'She doesn't even care about the prom!' Julia cried. 'She only wants to help because she fancies Jonny. He's probably the reason she's friends with Annie!'

'Yes, I know what you mean,' I agreed. Izzy was nodding her head too.

'So you don't need me now you have Dawn. I don't want to help any more.'

'But you have to!' Izzy sounded desperate. 'You're the one in charge of the stage set for the band to play on.'

'I've done the design, you just need to finish making it.'

'Please?' I begged, feeling as if things were just starting to slip out of our control.

'No. Dawn's a fake–I can see through her smiley, smiley face. She doesn't want me there,' Julia sniffed. 'She practically forced me to leave earlier to come and find the tiara even though it makes no difference whether we have it today or tomorrow. I couldn't say no—I would have looked like a loser. And Annie doesn't see it. No one sees it!'

'Look, we want you there. Please? Otherwise we're going to be stuck with smug Dawn until we leave and we'll never see you. Just ignore her. Annie is really nice and you should get to know her.'

'Is she?' Julia didn't sound convinced. 'There seems no point. After the prom's over, you two will just jet back to Paris and there'll be no reason for someone like me to be hanging around with someone like Annie.' She had a point. 'I really don't want to come back to the sleepover. It makes me feel . . . ek.'

'Ek?' Izzy asked, sounding puzzled. She sat down next to her mum on the bed.

'Like I don't . . . fit in.' Julia was twisting her hands and staring down at them. 'I wasn't at the same schools as everyone else in this year. We moved here just before senior school. Everyone was already in a clique.'

'Oh, that's hard,' I sympathized. 'It's bad enough going to a different junior school, but senior school is a whole different ball game.' Julia smiled gratefully at me.

'Come back with us and see how the evening is. At least now we know how we all feel!' Izzy pleaded. 'We need to stick together against Dawn!'

'No.' Julia had made up her mind. Izzy went white. I could tell from her twitching eye her brain was spiralling out of control, so before she could make things worse I Death Stared her, and waded in.

'Look, fair enough, don't come back to the sleepover—have a bit of a breather from Dawn, but please don't jump ship from the prom. We need you.'

Julia sighed, having no idea that her decision right now meant that we may or may not exist in the future. 'I don't know. I just want out.'

I wanted to scream. I thought Izzy was going to pass out.

'You'll miss out on all those brownie points from Jimpson if you leave. Please?' I practically choked. Izzy didn't speak.

She shrugged. 'I'll see how I feel tomorrow . . .'

'OK.' I gave in. 'How about we ask your mum where the tiara is?'

'Oh, sorry, love,' Julia's mum said when we asked her

downstairs. 'I gave that away a few years back when you stopped dressing up.'

'Thanks for being nice,' Julia said as she waved us off back to the sleepover. 'I'll see you tomorrow morning, Izzy?' Izzy nodded dumbly.

'It'll be OK,' I said to try and lighten the mood as we turned the corner.

'How will it?' Izzy said desperately. 'Mum isn't here, thanks to you telling her not to come back. If she pulls out of the prom, we may as well kiss goodbye to life as we know it.'

'Look, I couldn't force her to come. If we had gone on and on about it, she would have backed even further into the corner. We have to be careful. You saw how upset she was.'

'Yes, poor Mum,' Izzy agreed. 'I had no idea. It explains why she's so quiet.'

'We just have to hope she decides to stay on board.'

'And we still need to find the tiara. None of this matters at all if we don't find that.'

'Look, let's just go back to the sleepover and try not to think about the tiara for now. I think if it existed before, it will exist again—maybe it will just turn up via someone else. Maybe Dawn finds it—we don't know, do we?'

'OK, sorry. I'm just scared, Daisy.'

'Me too.' However, I was more than scared. I was terrified my dream would never come true. I just wanted to go back to my life in the future, but with Mum in it . . .

'So no tiara then?' Dawn said dripping with concern when we returned to find them both upstairs in Annie's bedroom. 'Bit of a wasted trip then, yeah?'

'Well, we have a week to find one or make one,' Annie said cheerfully. 'We'll be OK. Oh, where's Julia?'

'She didn't want to come back,' Izzy said quietly and glared at Dawn.

'Oh no, was it something I said?' Dawn joked bouncing up and down on Annie's bed. The floor was covered with camp beds and someone had dumped our bags on different ones. Dawn had made sure she was right next to Annie.

'She's not feeling great and wanted to go to bed,' I said, not wanting to give Dawn the satisfaction that she had anything to do with it.

'Oh, really?' Annie asked sympathetically. 'What's up? Is she OK?'

Before I could think up more tall stories Jonny bounced upstairs and poked his head round the door.

'Whoa! Girl overload! What's going on here? Mum said you wanted to see me when I got in.'

'We're having a sleepover!' Dawn said in a really girlie voice; I wanted to vom.

'Yes, we need to show you the stage plan,' I said, all business-like. 'We finalized it earlier. Can you let us know what you think?'

'Do I have to wear pink and put ribbons in my hair to join in?'

'Yes!' Dawn cried a bit too loudly.

'It's here,' Izzy said pulling it out of Julia's bag that she'd left behind. Jonny crept over all the beds, stepping on a packet of chocolate biscuits as he went, and crouched down next to her on the camp bed. 'We thought you could go there, if we arrange the fake forest around you to the left and the right? Would that work?'

'Wow, yes, it would. I totally love these drawings. Who did them?'

'Julia,' Izzy said proudly.

'Where is she? These are seriously impressive.'

'She's not feeling well.'

'That's a shame. Well, just tell her to make sure that we can have our cables at the back. That's the only thing that worries me. I don't want to be tripping over stuff.'

'Well, maybe we could do a different design?' Dawn butted her big nose in. 'To make it easier for you? We don't want to get in the way and ruin your performance.'

She carefully picked her way through the bedded floor to sit next to where Jonny was looking at the plans, like she was the stage manager or something. 'Is there anything *I* can do to help? I mean, I can take over if Julia isn't going to come back at all,' she simpered.

'Nah—this is great. I'm just saying about the cables, but I can help you set up on the day and show you what I mean. Julia's design is cool—keep it as it is. When we're famous, she can come and design all our stage sets!' Dawn looked like she was swallowing a really nasty sick burp. Suck it up, buttercup!

'Julia is coming back, isn't she?' Annie asked worriedly. 'She didn't say anything about dropping out, did she?'

'Of course she didn't!' I protested. 'She's just not well. Now who wants to play Truth or Dare?'

I had no idea how I was going to persuade Julia to change her mind. One thing I did know, she was the glue that held us all together—without her, we were scuppered.

Chapter eleven
Glory Days

'Morning, love. How was the sleepover? They all dead to the world?' Nana was making tea. It was Saturday morning and the sun was streaming into the kitchen and bouncing off the kettle blinding me. Panicky thoughts about the tiara and Julia's refusal to return to the prom had nervously greeted me when I awoke.

'Morning. Yes, just me up.'

'Tea?'

'Oh, thanks so much.'

'I think this prom idea is a good thing. Well done you for organizing it.'

'Thanks.'

'Annie's really enjoyed working on it, it's good for her to mix with different girls.' She practically whispered the last bit.

'Oh, what's wrong with her friends?' I asked surprised. Nana never seemed to say anything controversial like this. Apart from the time she had asked me what was going on with me and Izzy.

Nana: 'So, I see you've dropped Izzy in favour of this Celia.'

Me: 'Not really, we just drifted apart. She likes different things and so do I.'

Nana: 'Oh, I see. Shame, such a lovely girl, so is her mum. Well, don't burn your bridges, will you?'

I had remembered feeling unnerved at this, wondering if I'd made a huge mistake. But that soon disappeared when Celia invited me to her birthday and we became besties. I hadn't thought about Nana's little chat until now.

Meanwhile back in the Eighties Nana was looking thoughtful. 'Let's just say I've seen girls like that Dawn before—always out for themselves.' I must have looked shocked.

'The change in Annie this last week, making the costumes for the prom and hanging out with that lovely Julia girl, has been noticeable.'

'So how is Annie different?' I asked as of course I had no idea. All I knew was what I saw now and she seemed fine.

'She's moody usually. I think she knows her dad and I aren't fond of Dawn and her gang. Anyway, it's just lovely to see her sharing her interest with friends. It would be amazing for you all to keep in touch after you go home.' I was suddenly hit with a huge wave of sadness. I would like that too! Annie walked in just as Nana said that, making us both jump.

'I was thinking that as well, Mum,' she cried. 'We've only got a week left, Daisy, and then you go. It's gone so quick.'

'We're going to miss you,' Nana said fondly.

I had to blink continually for ages to batten down the hatches and stop my eyes from welling up.

'Well, luckily your dad and I are taking us all out for the day. We're going to go to Thorpe Park!'

'Did someone say we were going to Thorpe Park?' Jonny yawned as he wandered into the kitchen, scratching his head and looking like he'd invented bed hair.

'Yes, get dressed. We're going in an hour! Annie, go and wake the others, we need to get a move on!'

'That Julia's drawing is amazing,' Jonny said in the car.

'I know. I had no idea she was so good at art. She usually has her nose stuck in a book.' Annie said sounding surprised. 'I hope she's feeling better today.'

I wanted to join in the conversation but I was paralysed with fear by the lack of seatbelts in the back of the car. We were on a motorway and no one was strapped in. I felt like I was going to fly through the windscreen every time Grandpa touched the brakes.

'Why is no one scared about crashing?' I squeaked out through my clenched teeth, unable to take it any more.

'What do you mean?' Jonny asked, sounding amused. 'Dad's a safe driver.'

'But no one's wearing seatbelts! What if he brakes suddenly?'

'Put your arms out to cushion yourself,' Jonny said, as if I was an idiot.

'No, seriously, haven't you got adverts on telly telling you to belt up? It's so dangerous.'

Annie laughed. 'No one wears seatbelts in the back. Don't be ridiculous. It's totally safe.'

'It isn't! Everyone should wear them whether they're in the front or back.'

'I've never worn one in the back,' Jonny admitted.

'You're all mad!' I cried. 'Annie, promise me you'll always wear a seatbelt and be a really careful driver when you're older. Promise!' Nana laughed.

'Err, OK.' Annie was looking at me like I was one of those street preachers in the town centre telling everyone about The End of the World.

'I mean it,' I said urgently.

'Calm down,' Jonny laughed. 'We're not going to die!' Annie raised her eyebrows at me and shook her head. I was aware again of how I must look to her—like a hysterical stalker. I took a deep breath—I could change everything by telling her just one thing. I needed to appear normal if I ever wanted her to listen to me when the time came to warn her about the accident.

Thorpe Park was fun once I'd got over the trauma of the journey. It was a theme park though I have no idea what the theme was. Perhaps it was Lego Hair Land—there were so many solid hairdos (or rather don'ts!) and dodgy curly perms—the place was overrun!

'Let's go on the rollercoaster!' Annie cried as we spotted it from the entrance. I wasn't a great fan of them—they terrified me, but I didn't want to seem like a saddo. Maybe this time I could handle it . . .

When we settled into the seats and the guy rammed the safety neck brace thing over me, I started to feel sick and claustrophobic and the thought of throwing up everywhere gave me the mega fear.

'I want to get off,' I squeaked, just before we set off.

'What? Why? Are you OK?'

I shook my head.

'What is it?'

'I'm scared,' I managed to force out between gritted teeth. But it was too late; the ride had already started. Annie looked around wildly to see if she could find someone to help but our heads slammed against the back of our seats as we were propelled forwards up the steep slope. Why had I agreed to this?

'It'll be over before you know it. Look, hold my hand, squeeze as hard as you like.' I turned to look at her and she winked at me. 'It's fun!'

FUN????

I grabbed her hand across the seat and held it tight. I closed my eyes. Annie squeezed my fingers as we chugged up to the top of the slope.

'Any minute now!' she cried excitedly. 'Are you OK?' I nodded, keeping my eyes shut. If I didn't look then it wasn't happening. My stomach dipped signalling that we were jettisoning downwards, wind rushing in my face, the protective brace pressing on my chest making it hard to breathe.

'Arghhhh!' Annie cried, laughing. I grabbed her hand even harder and she pressed right back. Up we went again and what felt like upside down. 'Look, we're going to see the whole park!' Annie yelled and she crushed my fingers to make me open my eyes. I peeked. We were just about to reach the crest of the next slope. Annie put her other hand in the air and pulled my hand up so I had to do the same. 'Relax and let go!' she shouted. 'We're going dooooooooooown!!!' She started laughing uncontrollably and waving her hands in the air. I forgot how scared I was because I was laughing at her. I screamed as we plummeted down and Annie had her mouth wide open, pulling silly faces, still grasping my hand in the air. Out of nowhere the fear dispersed. I was on a rollercoaster with my mum. How could that be scary? She started screaming too, louder than me and started whooping at the same time. Uncle Jonny joined in from the carriage behind. We were all going nuts. The rollercoaster went loop the loop, and we screamed even more, almost choking from laughing and screaming at the same time. My tummy was in my mouth but I was OK with it. Mum held my hand and never let go. When the ride finished, tears were streaming down my face, not from crying, but from laughing. The safety braces lifted automatically over our heads and we were free to go.

'How was that? You survived OK!' Annie gasped, wiping the tears off her cheeks. 'Now don't tell me that wasn't fun!'

'Yes it was. Thank you.' And I grabbed her hand and squeezed it, not caring if I came across as a stalker. She grinned and then Uncle Jonny jumped in between us.

'Ladies, race you to the ghost train!'

'Come on!' Annie yelled. 'He's got a head start!'

Later on, eating lunch on the grass in one of the park areas, I wished I had my phone. Not to text anyone, or share it on Instagram or Snapchat, but just to take a picture of my family. For once it felt almost whole. I made a decision to look Uncle Jonny up when we got back, say hi, whether he liked it or not . . .

'You gonna eat that?' he asked me as I daydreamed, holding my sandwich.

'Yes! Hands off!'

'Make me!' And he grabbed it and ran off.

'Come on, don't let him get away with that!' Annie laughed and we chased him all round the grass until Annie jumped on his back and I tickled him to death.

'I've licked it, you can't have it!'

'That's not the point!' I yelled. He dropped it and I stood on it by accident.

'I've gone off it now. You can have it back!'

The day was perfect. I felt as if Annie and I had had some quality time. But somehow, it still wasn't enough—it never would be.

I fell asleep on the way back, my head resting on Annie's shoulders, all thoughts of being mangled in a car wreck abandoned. I dreamed about Celia being here instead of Izzy. She bossed everyone about and ended up being best friends with Dawn. In the dream Annie wasn't a girl but she was like Nana, and she looked like my shadowy vision I have of her from photos and the last few remaining memories. I told her about the future and she promised to make sure she didn't die.

'We're here! Wake up, sleepy-head,' Annie said in my ear. 'You were dribbling!'

'Nice.' I yawned. I rubbed my eyes and climbed out of the car. I could feel the ghost of the dream following me, adding weight to my idea of telling Annie about the future. I didn't care what Izzy said. This was my life, not hers and it was part of The Plan. I just needed to think of a way of doing it so no Butterfly Effect happened . . .

'Why don't you just keep your bed in here for the rest of the week?' Annie suggested at bedtime. I was so happy I could barely speak. I just nodded. Today had been perfect. The only person missing had been Dad . . .

CHApter twelve
Things Can Only Get Better

Monday morning jitters. What if Julia was no longer part of Team Prom? She and Izzy were due any second to walk to school.

'You left your toast,' Uncle Jonny shouted at me as I walked out of the kitchen to wait by the front door. 'Can I eat it?'

'Yes sure, knock yourself out.' I couldn't face food.

The doorbell rang and I jumped, whipping the door open, revealing a Death Staring Izzy shaking her head. I knew then that Julia had resigned.

'So, did you have a good weekend?' I asked in an over-the-top voice, trying to disguise my overwhelming disappointment.

'Yes,' Izzy said dully. 'We went to the seaside. It was really sunny.' I could tell it was an effort for her to be normal. She must be going bananas in her head. This was dire.

'Do you want to come in? Annie's just brushing her

teeth.' Izzy nodded and traipsed into the hall, plonking herself down on the stairs. She looked like all the life had been punched out of her. I tried to make eye contact with Julia, but she wouldn't look at me. You're making a HUGE mistake, I wanted to yell.

'Hey,' Annie called as she trotted down the stairs, squeezing past Izzy, 'are you feeling better?'

'Yes thanks,' Julia replied going bright red. 'Look, I don't want—'

'Heeeeey! Julia, loved your designs for the prom,' Jonny swaggered into the hallway crunching the last corner of my Marmite toast. 'So have you already started making the actual forest yet?'

'Er, no, we were er . . . decorating the thrones last week . . .' Julia stammered out.

'I can't wait to see what the stage set's going to look like. If you want help moving everything once it's finished just let me know, yeah?'

'Errr . . . OK. Thanks.'

'Listen, I wouldn't be surprised after this if the drama department don't want you to help with all the school plays in future. They would love how you design stuff,' Annie said enthusiastically and winked at Julia making her blush crimson on top of her already mottled face.

'I'm off to school—you girls going to join me?' Jonny asked.

'Yes, come on girls, school awaits.' Annie grabbed her bag and followed Jonny out of the door. 'So we're doing the forest today?' Annie asked no one in particular. 'Julia, what do you think of asking Miss Avery to intervene and get us off English after lunch? Then we can have a good stretch of making stuff.'

Julia didn't say anything for ages and I was waiting for her to refuse. My heart was thumping in my ears. I held my breath.

'I er . . . guess that would be good,' she replied finally. I let out a huge gasp of breath and looked at Izzy—she shrugged like she was confused.

'So you're full steam ahead with Team Prom?' I asked Julia tentatively.

She flinched, hesitating. Eventually she said, 'It would seem so, yes.'

'Great! Now, what colour should we do the flowers?' and Annie grabbed Julia's arm, linked in with her and off they went up the street trailing in Jonny's wake.

'OMG, what's going on?' I asked Izzy.

'Until about five minutes ago she wasn't doing it any more.' Izzy sounded stunned. 'She was adamant.'

When we got in from school that afternoon, Nana had left a note on the kitchen table.

'She wants us to go the shops and get something for dinner,' Annie said, scanning it. 'She's left a list.'

When we'd finished at the supermarket, I spotted a photo booth by the exit.

'Come on, let's get our picture taken,' I urged Annie. 'I have some spare coins.' I'd secreted some from the petty cash which I would replace when the ticket sales came in. Izzy didn't want any photographic evidence of us being here, but she wouldn't know about this!

'Yes—I love those things. We can pull silly faces!' We raced over with our bulging shopping bags and drew back the curtain. 'Sit on my knee and I can poke my head over your shoulder. Ready?' I nodded. 'We're not allowed to look normal!'

'I'm blind!' I cried after the first flash, gurning for the camera.

'You're not trying hard enough!' Annie cried. 'Look hideous!'

She was pulling grotesque faces, curling her tongue and making pig noises. I could see it all reflected in the glass. It just made me laugh.

'Right, that's it, you're getting punished!' She laughed as I failed to look as ugly as her. Annie started tickling me, so for the next two photos I was screaming hysterically.

'I think I'm going to wet myself. Stop!'

'Urgh! Not all over my legs!' But she didn't stop and I could hardly catch my breath I was laughing so much.

We fell out of the booth giggling and I leaned against it with my legs crossed trying hard not to pee my pants.

'There's a loo round the corner,' Annie said and I gratefully raced while she waited for the photos.

'Let me see, let me see!' You could only make out it was me in one of the photos, but only just. I was pulling a thicky-no-brain face. In all the others Annie was pulling daft faces and I was so hysterical that I was out of focus. I handed them back to her.

'No, keep them. You paid for them.' So I ripped them in half and we had two photos each.

'Let's share them, and we can both remember that I nearly weed all over your legs.'

'Wow, a proper moment to treasure. Thanks!'

'You're welcome. Come on, we better get home before the ice cream melts.'

I stashed away my precious photos in my bag. They were definitely coming back home with me.

That evening Annie and I sat sewing till late. There

was the school trip to London tomorrow and we had to make up for lost time.

'Has your dad met anyone else?' Annie suddenly asked out of the blue.

'Why do you ask that?' It took me by total surprise.

'I don't know. It just popped into my head. You don't talk much about home.'

'Yes, he has met someone else, Mary, The Interloper,' I said dully.

'And I'm guessing you don't like her?'

'How can you tell?' I asked sarcastically.

'Is she dreadful?'

'I just don't like her.'

'Why?'

I pulled a face I could never ever explain this part.

'What does Celia say about it?' Annie asked.

'She thinks I'm mad because Dad and I had a terrible fight about going on holiday with Mary and her kids and I said I didn't want to go. That was the last time I spoke to Dad, and then we came here.' It felt really odd talking to Mum about this stuff.

'So you had an argument the day before you travelled here?'

I nodded. Poor Dad. What if I never made it back home? What if his last memory of me was those things

I'd said? Eurgh . . . I shook my head to banish the thought.

'Celia thought you were mad because of why exactly?'

'Because everyone wants a free holiday, surely? She doesn't really do heart to hearts.'

Annie furrowed her brow. 'Why don't you ring him now and say sorry?'

I thanked the law of time travel that we had fallen into a technology desert. Back home, there was no excuse not to ring or text a parent. All of us were practically stalked by satellites or something ridiculous like that. But lying to say where you were and what you'd been up to was so hard when someone could post a pic online of you somewhere you shouldn't be. Me: 'I was just at Celia's doing homework.' Dad: 'Then how come there're pictures all over the net of you dancing on a table dressed as a pineapple?'

'He's away on business now, and I can't get hold of him till he gets back, just after we get home.'

'Oh, that's a shame. I'm sure he'll have forgotten all about it though.' I nodded, but I couldn't forget it. No amount of shaking my head and silently singing LA-LA-LA could remove the stain of the argument from my brain. The business of the last week had kind of bleached it out for a bit, but like a stubborn Bolognaise sauce splodge, it wilfully resisted all sorts of wiping.

'Why doesn't Celia do heart to hearts?'

'I don't know. It's not her thing. I don't really talk to her about stuff like that.'

'Maybe you should?'

I shrugged. I had tried and failed. No point. It was just the way it was.

'Don't you talk to Izzy? She would listen.'

I sat there, material in my hands, screwing it into my fists. 'We used to be best friends. But we kind of drifted apart over the last year, different friendship groups, that sort of thing.'

'Oh, that's sad. But you guys seem to be friends now, right?'

I looked at my hands. I didn't know what we were . . .

'Is Mary nice to you?' Annie asked, maybe sensing Izzy wasn't a good subject to cover.

'Yes. Too nice.'

'How can you be too nice? Surely that's better than being horrible?' Annie laughed. 'She's probably trying to make friends.'

'Well, I don't want her to!' I retorted hotly, tears sneaking up behind my eyes from nowhere. Dammit! 'I don't need another mum.' I just want you, I thought.

Annie reached her hand over the table and squeezed my solid fist. As I smiled at her through the mist, a flashback hit me like a freight train—Mum and me dancing at a party, years and years ago. It must have been just before she died. She was wearing a red dress and was swinging me round to some music. Dad came and joined in and put his arms round both of us so I was sandwiched between them, my face pressed into Mum's chest. Annie looked intently at me and I could see the woman she was going to be: beautiful and kind. My mum. It was too much and I stood up abruptly and left the table, tears coming properly now. I made it to the bathroom before my heart felt like it was going to explode and everything just came flooding out. Why couldn't I have come back in time to when I was little? So that she could be my mum properly? It wasn't fair! I felt like my heart was going to break. I couldn't breathe, the sobs were so violent. I wanted all this to feel different, for Annie to feel like my mum . . .

Slumped on the bathroom floor I was a mess. Snot was bubbling out of my nose and sliming down my top lip. Crying was so unglamorous!

There was a knock on the door. I hadn't locked it in my haste to collapse and it opened. Nana stood there with Annie hovering behind her looking really worried.

'Hey, what's all this?' Nana said kindly. 'Annie said you were upset.' She got down on her knees. 'Pass us the loo roll, Annie.' She did. 'Blow your nose.' I did as I was told. Nana gave me a hug, something I was used to. Her smell was so familiar and safe that the sobs started subsiding almost immediately.

'Do you want to talk about it?' Nana asked. 'Annie was ever so worried she'd upset you.'

'No, she hasn't done anything. I just had a . . . a . . . memory of my mum and I hadn't thought about it for years and it kind of got to me.'

'Oh, phew!' Annie said sounding relieved. 'When we were talking I thought it was because I mentioned your dad's girlfriend when you don't like her.'

I shook my head. 'No she doesn't upset me. Just makes me . . . cross. I don't want her there.'

'Well, that's understandable, love. You've had him to yourself. Is she his first since your mum died?' I nodded. 'It's going to be hard.'

'I would hate Dad to meet someone else if you died!' Annie said fiercely in support of me.

'But what if Dad was lonely?' Nana said reasonably. 'What if he was so sad by himself? Tired of being on his own? I wouldn't want that, would you?'

'No, I suppose not,' Annie admitted. 'You're right.

Dad would be rubbish on his own. And drive Jonny and me mental. So I would probably go out looking for a wife for him!' I laughed.

'Look, Daisy, does she make your dad happy?' Nana asked me gently.

'I guess,' I reluctantly agreed.

'And you want him to be happy?' I nodded. 'Then that's a start.' She ruffled my hair. 'I think you two need to go to bed. It's a long day tomorrow.'

Lying in the darkness after my meltdown I wondered how to frame what I needed to say without causing a time avalanche that would obliterate everything in the future.

'What do you want to be when you grow up?' Annie asked yawning.

'Something to do with fashion. A designer maybe?'

'Oh, me too. I love fashion and sewing and making things.' I almost blurted out that she should become a designer instead, never become a stylist, but remembered what Izzy had said about the Butterfly Effect: if she wasn't a stylist, then she and Julia wouldn't meet mine or Izzy's dad on the famous night out. Meaning we wouldn't exist. It was like skipping through a virtual minefield of words—one wrong turn of phrase or suggestion, and puff! I could be snuffed out in the future, just because of something I said in 1985. Argh!

'I want to go to fashion college when I leave school,' I said instead. 'Like my mum.'

'You should! All those bags you make sound amazing. Would you make me one before you leave? I have lots of spare material.'

'Yes, no probs. I can knock one up in no time.'

'Oh thanks, that would be so cool.' She paused and I was about to butt in when . . . 'Something you said earlier made me think about stuff.'

'Oh, what?' I turned my head on the camp bed to try and see her face in the murky darkness, but all I could make out was the inky outline of her body under the duvet.

'I was thinking about Mary. Does she have kids of her own?'

'Yes, Ben and Elizabeth. They're both younger than me.'

'So she will be a mum to them already. She doesn't *need* to be a mum to you.'

'I know.' That was exactly what Dad had said.

'So if Mary isn't horrid and she's never going to try and be your mum, how about seeing what she's really like? You know, without getting cross or hiding in your room?'

'I still might not like her,' I retorted stubbornly.

'But what if you do like her? You don't have to be best friends. Just see how it goes?'

I couldn't speak because I didn't want to have to do any of that, because what I wanted was for Mum to be alive when I got back home. A single tear escaped from the corner of my eye and slid into my ear.

'Daisy, sorry, did I say too much?'

I rubbed my eyes and took a deep breath.

'No, I guess I've never properly talked to anyone about it before.'

'I like talking. Sometimes I wish Dawn liked deep and meaningfuls. Still, you can't have everything!'

'No, you can't,' I agreed, thinking of Celia.

'You're very easy to talk to. I feel like I could tell you anything.'

My stomach turned a somersault after Annie said that and a warm glow flooded through my body, my anxiety about Mary momentarily forgotten. I think my face was burning—I was glad it was dark! I wished, wished, *wished* that this could happen again, but not in 1985, at home. 'Thanks, Annie. You're very easy to talk to as well.' I spotted an opening for something else. 'I reckon Julia would be a good person to chat to. You probably have more in common than you think.'

'Yeah, perhaps you're right. I never knew she was so

good at design. She's a dark horse. I'll see if she wants to sit with me on the coach tomorrow.' She paused briefly. 'Will you promise to write when you get home to Paris? Pen pals would be cheaper than phoning. You can let me know how you're getting on with Mary. If you feel really bad you can always ring me. Ask your dad first though because it'll be expensive.'

'Pen pals?' I had no idea what she was talking about.

'Write letters, you dur brain!'

'Oh, snail mail! Yes, of course.'

'Do you call it that because you all eat snails in France?'

'Ewww, no! I don't! Gross!' We laughed for a bit and when there was a lull in the giggles I lay really quiet and an idea popped into my head that I felt was a genius way of explaining what I needed to say without appearing too crazy. I rehearsed it in my head before I spoke.

'Annie?' I whispered in the gloom.

'Mmmm?' she answered back.

'I need to tell you something.' I spoke quietly, my words feeling like beacons of hope. 'Please don't think I'm being a loon, but I keep having a recurring dream about something. If I don't tell you about it, I'll never forgive myself.'

Silence.

'Annie?' Her outline remained still, and then I heard a gentle snore. I scrambled off the camp bed and leaned over her. She was asleep.

'Annie, wake up!' I hissed. She was passed out and shaking her awake would look like I was a desperate sad super stalker. I gave up for now and tried to sleep—but the idea buzzed round like a trapped fly hell-bent on escaping my head . . .

Annie's face loomed over me as she prodded me. 'Here, I made you a cup of tea and some toast.' I sat up and yawned; she was perched on the end of the camp bed in her nightie. The stripy curtains had been drawn so their dazzling monochrome wasn't quite so offensive on the eye. It was cloudy outside.

'Wow, thanks, Annie! I don't think Dad has ever made me breakfast in bed before. You're the best!'

'I'm so sorry about making you so upset last night. I can't imagine what it must be like to lose your mum. I think I would always be sad for the rest of my life if that happened to me.'

'It wasn't your fault. It just happens sometimes. Don't worry about it.'

'Are you sure? I felt awful when I woke up and remembered all over again.'

'I'm sure. Honestly.'

'If you ever need to talk about it, I promise I'll listen.' Annie smiled. 'I think you're so strong after what you've been through.'

I didn't feel strong. 'Thanks, Annie. That's really sweet of you.' I felt very touched. 'Listen I wanted to tell you—'

'Annie, Daisy—the shower's free. You'd better get a move on!' Nana said, poking her head round the door. 'Now, I'm going to do sandwiches for the school trip today. Is cheese and Marmite OK?' We both nodded.

'Thanks, Mum. I'm going to jump in the shower before Jonny hogs it.' Annie leaped up and disappeared through the door. I sighed. Maybe when we're in London I could warn Annie then. While I wondered how I could get her on her own, another idea pinged into my head. Maybe we had been looking in the wrong place for the tiara the entire time. Maybe it had never been in Kingston after all . . . Time to implement the next point in Operation Hairspray, even if point three hadn't been ticked off yet:

4. Find the tiara—our ticket home

Chapter thirteen
The Search Is Over

There was an ear-splitting screech as Mrs Northwood, the art teacher, fiddled with the volume on the coach microphone. We all groaned, covering our ears. 'We will be getting off in a bit to look at the National Gallery. After we've all had the tour, you'll have a chance to eat your packed lunch in the area reserved for school parties. Then for the last hour and a half, you're free to wander round the gallery some more, or go into the National Portrait Gallery or wander into China Town or Covent Garden. I'll show you where the coach will be for a two-thirty departure back to school.'

'I say we go and check out China Town!' Annie whispered through the gap in the coach seat where she sat with Julia, hopefully becoming best friends!

'OK,' Izzy agreed. I noticed she was wearing a really beautiful intricately beaded bracelet.

'Where did you get that?'

'Julia made it. It's amazing, isn't it? She's so clever.'

'You're kidding? It's totally gorgeous.'

'She showed me how she does them—she's got all the beads and everything. I told her she should sell them at school.'

'She totally should. Hey, maybe you should get her to make one for the prom queen. That would go down really well with Annie.'

'What a great idea.'

'Look, I think we need to sneak off on our own. I've got the petty cash from the prom fund.'

Izzy stared at me looking puzzled. 'Why? What for?'

'The tiara. We're totally running out of time. We're going to not . . . you know, exist unless we find it. And I have a gut feeling we might find it here. It's obviously not in Kingston anywhere.' This was kind of our last chance. I had no idea what we would do if we came home empty handed . . . Where else could it be?

'How are we going to lose this lot?' And she nodded her head towards the mums and Dawn.

'I don't know yet . . .'

When it was lunch, Dawn raced ahead and bagged a table with some other kids with only a space left for Annie. The communal room was rammed with children from different schools, all on day trips to visit the gallery.

'I bet you could squeeze on their table if you took a

chair over,' Izzy suggested kindly to Julia as we looked around for somewhere to sit. 'It doesn't look too cramped there.'

'No way. Have you seen how weird and clingy Dawn's being? If I so much as look at Annie, she starts trying to drag her off,' Julia protested. 'I've had enough. If Annie wants to hang out with Dawn, she's welcome to her. I'm just going to do my bit with the prom and after it's over, that's it. No more Dawn and no more Annie.'

'But you have so much in common!' Izzy cried in dismay.

'She doesn't seem to think so. I can do without the hassle.'

'But after what you said last week, I thought you wanted to make friends.'

Julia eyed Izzy suspiciously. 'What's going on? Why are you so keen for Annie and I to be friends? *You*'re being all weird about it too.'

'I'm not,' Izzy blustered. 'I just think it's a shame when you get on so well.'

'But Dawn's always going to stick her nose in. Look, I'm going over there. I can see a space. I'll see you after lunch. We're going to China Town, aren't we? I want to get some Chinese lanterns for the stage.' Izzy nodded.

'Hey, we could sneak out now,' I said after Julia left.

'Tell the teachers we've finished our lunch and no one will ever know. Say we got lost or something which is why we didn't meet the others.'

Izzy hesitated. 'OK.'

Outside the gallery I checked the photocopied A-Z map Mrs Northwood had given us. (Googlemaps for the Eighties!) 'China town is that way, I think.' Back in the future, there was no way any kid would be allowed to sneak off into the surrounding area without at least two adults, a satellite tracking system and an embarrassing day-glow school tabard. Times had certainly changed!

After we'd wandered vaguely in the right direction past fascinating Asian supermarkets, cramped-looking restaurants with spit-roasting ducks rotating in the windows, and Chinese newsagents, we found ourselves on a side street between an old man's pub and a bakery.

'Is that Prince William? He's a toddler here. Weird!' Izzy pointed to one of the Royal Family memorabilia displays outside a touristy shop.

'We better get a move on,' I said spotting a clock in the shop window. 'We've only got half an hour left.'

'What are we looking for, exactly?' Izzy moaned as we traipsed down the street, tripping on the cobbles that had started sprouting like weeds through the tarmac. 'We just seem to be walking aimlessly.'

'Ye Olde Curiosity Shoppe!' I cried. 'What did you think we were looking for?'

'OK, keep your wig on. I haven't seen it yet. Or anything like it at all.' She was right. It was looking less and less likely and we would soon have to return to the coach, assuming we could find the way back.

The street suddenly curved to the right and there was a brick archway above us drawing the two buildings opposite each other together so they were almost touching. The road started to slope down slightly with the surface now completely cobbled. I looked back and could see all the touristy shops looming behind us just round the bend, but something made me continue along the cobbles.

'Should we turn back?' Izzy asked nervously. 'This street feels a bit . . . odd.'

'Let's just see what's all the way round here and then we'll go back.'

'OK.' We carried on, walking carefully now on the cobbles. There wasn't really a pavement to cling to. The buildings seemed to stretch right up to the sky and the street turned into an alleyway. It felt like someone had turned down the lights.

'What's that place?' Izzy asked in a hushed tone and pointed ahead. On the right, set back from the rest of the buildings, was a shop with a little flag-stoned front patio and creaky wrought-iron gate. It looked so out of place compared to all the other buildings.

'Let's go and see.' As we got closer I could see all sorts of glittery things and props and party paraphernalia displayed in the bay window. Izzy had already pushed open the gate and walked up to the door, peering inside. You couldn't read the sign from outside of the gate, where I was still standing just gaping at the place. The lettering was all worn away. The sign itself hung sideways from the front of the building over the front door like signs you might see in Victorian times, or traditional pub signs.

Izzy walked round to the other side of the sign and looked up. 'Come here a sec,' she said to me, pulling a face.

I slipped through the gate and met her underneath it. I looked up to see what she was looking at. The sign read:

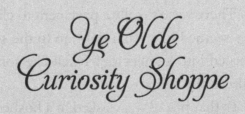

'NO WAY!' I yelled. 'It can't be!' Relief flooded through me.

'Let's hope the tiara is still here, and not stuck in the future after all,' Izzy said nervously.

I pushed open the door and a bell jangled above, making us both jump. The shop was rammed with glitter and sparkle and old bar signs, ships in bottles, kitsch Jesus statues, cutesy photo frames, and a whole section of books on tarot cards and magic. It was an amazing shop. It was how I'd imagined it to look when I'd conjured up an image of it after I had seen the lettering on the bag way back in the PE cupboard.

The shop was deserted and eerily silent. I picked up a pair of gold glittery stiletto shoes that were placed next to some long gold satin gloves—no prices on either of them. Izzy had disappeared somewhere at the back.

'Daisy,' she squeaked. 'Come here!' I followed the sound of her voice and found her in the middle of a seating area where you could try on clothes. She was pointing to a shelf above a clothes rack. On a red velvet cushion the tiara sat majestically, sparkling and radiating light like a disco ball.

'Wow,' I breathed. 'It's even more amazing than I remembered. I wonder how much it is?'

'How much have you got?' a voice said from behind

me. I jumped and spun round. A small Chinese man had somehow manoeuvred right there without me having the slightest clue. His accent threw me completely—it was very thick Scottish.

'Err, I don't know,' Izzy gasped and gave me a Death Stare.

I scrabbled around in my bag to find the kitty envelope. 'Fifteen pounds,' I said despondently, knowing a tiara this amazing would cost at least three times that.

'Is that really all you have?' he asked, his eyes twinkling, the tiara making them glimmer even more. I nodded. I didn't know what to say. What if he said it wasn't enough? I *knew* it wasn't enough.

'Look, we need the tiara,' Izzy pleaded desperately. 'All we have in the entire world is the money in that envelope. You don't understand what buying this means to us.'

'Oh, I understand all right...' He raised his eyebrows and smiled. 'I'm just not sure *you* really understand.'

'Have we got enough money?' I asked, my heart in my mouth.

'What do *you* think the tiara's worth?'

'Probably a lot more than we have,' I said truthfully, sensing we weren't going to get it.

He nodded. 'You're right, young lady.'

My shoulders involuntarily drooped; this felt

hopeless. How on earth were we ever going to find extra money now when we had to be back at the coach stop in about ten minutes?

'We just need it, OK?' Izzy said quietly, a tear running down her face. 'I can't magic money from nowhere. I don't even know how much extra.' She looked defeated.

'I know you won't believe us,' I said to the man giving it one last attempt, looking right into his hypnotic eyes, 'but our lives depend on that tiara. I'm not even exaggerating.' If it had been nearer, I would have snatched it and run.

'Let's just go,' Izzy said flatly after a few moments of him just smiling beatifically at us. 'What's the point?' And she pushed past the man and me in order to leave.

I grabbed her hand. I wasn't going to give up that easily.

'Stay, Izzy. There must be something we can do. Let me look in my bag.' I scrabbled around and pulled out the little notebook we used for prom ideas. The photos of Annie and I dropped and fell on the floor.

'What's that?' the man asked curiously. I picked it up hurriedly.

'Nothing.' He stared right at me. It felt like he could see everything going on inside my head. I started to feel dizzy, a bit like I had in the PE cupboard.

'You have enough now.'

'For what?' Izzy asked sounding confused.

'For the tiara.'

'How?' I said, the spins receding.

He tapped the side of his nose mysteriously. 'You *do* understand.'

'Understand what?' Izzy asked, her eyes wide.

'That there's more to the tiara than meets the eye . . . Now, would you like a bag?' I nodded. He shuffled over to the shelf and reached up, grabbed the tiara and took it to the till on the left. I followed him.

'Here you go,' and he handed me the familiar Ye Olde Curiosity Shoppe bag. I took it and passed him the money. He shook his head.

'We need to pay,' I stated.

'I told you, you had enough.'

'Really?' Izzy questioned, screwing her face up in a puzzled manner. 'But—'

'Remember, treat the tiara wisely. And don't forget, home is *always* where the heart is. Goodbye.' And he retreated, still smiling, into the doorway behind the till which was covered by a jangling multi-coloured beaded curtain.

We ran outside the shop and burst into excited squeals. Izzy hugged me.

'What on earth happened there?' Izzy gasped.

'I don't know. He totally freaked me out though.'

'Me too. Do you think he knows the tiara is *magic*?'

'He must. Or he can do magic or something whacko like that. Why else would he say all that?' Izzy shrugged. 'Quick,' I hissed, 'let's go before he changes his mind.'

'What time is it?' Izzy puffed.

'No idea, but I reckon we're going to be late unless we get a wiggle on.' Running up the incline round the bend and out into the central bit of China Town, the quietness of the shop seemed far behind us. Before we dived into the melee of tourist central, I glanced over my shoulder to the street we'd just left and couldn't see where we'd been. The bend in the road didn't seem to be there. I shook my head—I must have been imagining things. But before I could look again, a lorry pulled up and parked in front of the bakery, blocking the view.

'Daisy!' Izzy called. 'Get a move on.'

A trick of the light, I reasoned and followed Izzy into the crowds.

We raced all the way, crashing into people, turning the wrong way twice, finally making it to the front steps of the gallery.

'The bus stop's round here to the left,' Izzy cried. And sure enough, there was the coach, with Mrs Northwood pacing up and down outside.

'Where have you been?' she shouted. 'You're not even on the list—we almost left without you! It's only because your friends said you were missing that we stayed at all. Get on, both of you.'

We clambered up the steps, the engine firing up as we did so. Annie had saved us two spaces behind her and Dawn. Julia was sat behind us on her own looking a bit left out.

'Where did you go?' Annie asked looking concerned. 'I've been so worried.'

'We went for a bit of a wander to find souvenir tat and ended up getting really lost,' I explained, trying to sound convincing, but still feeling somewhat dazed. I couldn't get what had just happened out of my head. The tiara MUST be magic. And was everything else in that shop magic too? I wondered what the glittery shoes did.

'What I don't understand,' said Dawn in her best detective's voice, 'is why you're not on the class list.' She gave me a fake worried look.

'A mix-up,' I answered a bit lamely.

'What, like the mix-up about you staying with Annie

and Julia instead of the other two girls?' she asked interestedly.

'Yes, exactly that,' Izzy piped up.

'Anyway it doesn't matter; look what we found on our travels.' And I produced the tiara from the bag.

Point Four of Operation Hairspray struck off.

4. Find the tiara—our ticket home ✓

'Oh, wow, it's beautiful,' Annie cooed.

'So delicate,' Julia gushed, poking her head between the seats. 'Well done, you two!'

'Can I try it on?' Dawn asked leaning over to try and grab it.

'No!!!!!' both Izzy and I practically screamed.

'Hey, no need to shout. I was just asking.' She slumped back against the coach seat.

'Sorry,' I said. 'It just cost so much money we don't want to break it.'

'Like I would break it!' Dawn said crossly and settled back in her seat, every now and then sneaking suspicious glances at us through the seats, which totally unnerved me. It felt like she was up to something . . .

Chapter Fourteen
Everything She Wants

'Did you finish the outfits last night?' Julia asked Annie as we walked to school on Wednesday morning. The prom was on mega countdown now—only two days to go. 'You know I can make you a necklace for the queen to match the colour. What do you think?' I looked at Izzy and she grinned at me.

'Oh that sounds like a great idea—you are full of little surprises!' I felt relieved that the mums seemed to at least be talking after Dawn hijacked Annie yesterday. 'Yes, we've just got a few little things to add, but the outfits are done,' Annie replied, looking pleased. 'I was so tired that I almost fell asleep on the sewing machine. I could hardly talk—Daisy practically had to carry me to bed!' I nodded in agreement, and a fluttery anxious sensation resumed residence in my tummy. I never seemed to find the right time to talk to her about the future.

When we arrived at school, Dawn was nowhere to be seen. She wasn't in her usual place by the gates ready to drag Annie off. We trudged round to the playground and I noticed her talking to some of the exchange kids on the other side. She spotted us and jogged over just as the bell rang.

'Morning!' she cried cheerily looking like she'd won the Lotto.

'Hey,' Annie replied. 'How come you're here so early?'

'Just doing some research,' and she looked directly at me and raised her eyebrows, smiling in a sick-inducing way. 'Come on, Annie, let's go. It's the results today. I wonder *who* will be nominated?' And she grabbed her arm to drag her to form room and away from us.

'Wait for the others,' Annie cried. 'Come on, Julia!' And she dug her heels in until we caught up. Instead of resisting and ignoring Annie, Dawn listened.

'Sure, no probs. Team Prom all together!'

Just when you thought you knew what she was up to, she would play a different game. It was like cat and mouse.

'Where will the results be put up?' Julia asked at lunchtime as we rushed out of the classroom, regrouping in the corridor.

'Outside the office, I think,' Annie replied.

As we approached the office noticeboard, people

were beginning to gather round, but there was nothing to report. No results were posted yet. Dawn rocked up a few moments later.

'Well, ladies, this is it,' she said eagerly. 'Who's going to wear the amaaaaaazing tiara?'

Just then the side door to the office opened and out came Glasses Lady.

'Ooooh, quite a crowd!' she tittered, fluffing up her hair into even more of a bouffant. 'It's all very exciting.'

'Wow, there's lots of interest!' Annie said looking around in amazement. 'Mr Sheppard's discos never got this kind of attention!'

'Who's she?' I heard someone ask her friend looking at the results paper on the board. 'She's not in the Fifth Year, is she?' Ridiculous hairdos were blocking my view of the noticeboard.

'No idea.'

'Oh, good, Jonny West has made the shortlist for king—I'm definitely voting for him!' someone cried excitedly.

'Ooooh, me too!' another girl joined in, and soon there was a chorus of voices all demonstrating the very same. Jonny, the reluctant king . . .

I *still* couldn't read anything, but somehow managed to shove to the front. Izzy was squeezed in next to me.

'I don't believe it,' Izzy hissed. 'Have you seen that?' I nodded disbelievingly.

There, in black-and-white old-fashioned type-written text, was Dawn's name in the list of nominees for queen!

'How do you think she's on the list?' I whispered to Izzy in the lunch queue later on. 'She must have cheated. No one would vote for a Second Year. The other two are Fifth Years . . .'

'Who knows? It makes no difference to us how she did it. The fact is, she's got a nomination. All we have to do is make sure the mums stay as close as they can and then we run off with the tiara and go back to our *normal* lives.' She sounded really sad when she said that.

'What's up?' I asked confused. 'I thought you'd be glad to go back home.'

'Oh, I am. It'll just be weird. You know . . .'

She caught me off guard. I'd been so busy thinking about when to warn Annie about the future and sorting the prom, that I hadn't thought what would happen to Izzy and me when we got home.

'Yes, it will be weird.' Lame response, Daisy!

'Come on, the girls have saved us a place.' Izzy paid and left me hanging by the till . . .

That afternoon, standing in the scorching sun

fielding during rounders, I made a major decision about warning Annie. I was terrified of her thinking I was a fruit loop and ruining the last few days I had in the Eighties with her, so I would tell her on the morning of the prom instead. Having come to that conclusion, I felt like I could relax and enjoy the final prep now we had found the tiara. Everything felt like it was working out perfectly. I couldn't see what could go wrong.

During a lull in the game where the ball kept whizzing to the other side of the field, Dawn, who was fielding with me, casually wandered over. I felt the hairs stand to attention on the back of my neck in some sort of high-alert warning.

'So, how's it going?' she asked all syrupy.

'Errr, good. Why?'

'Just wondered how you were finding the *exchange*?' And she over-pronounced the word exchange.

'Yeah, it's great.'

'So is this school very different from your one in France?' Her eyes were boring into mine and she was fluttering her electric blue eyelashes, to distract me before she stung me with some sort of poisonous barbed comment, just like a scorpion.

'Errr, yes. It's completely different . . .'

'How different? I'd *love* you to tell me.'

'Well, everyone's from different countries and we learn different stuff than here and—'

'Catch!' someone shouted as a ball came flying our way. I made a pathetic attempt, dropped it, and then threw it back where it fell short by a long way. I was never going to be an Olympic rounders player, if there was such a thing.

'Look, I'm not really interested in your school,' Dawn continued smiling. No kidding. 'I know you're not even from there.'

'What?' I choked, trying not to let the fear creep into my voice. Which was hard as my heart was pounding so hard, it was trying to leap out of my ribcage.

'Yes, I did a bit of investigating this morning after your names were mysteriously "missed off" the trip list yesterday. I spoke to the two Americans who were supposed to have been staying with Annie and Julia and they said they'd never seen you or Izzy before this exchange and maybe you were from this school instead. They were utterly confused as to who you really were.'

'We are from that school!'

'Really? Shall I go and ask them then? I think they're on another rounders pitch. They weren't very happy at being lumped with Sharon Day as their host.' She arched her eyebrows and smirked slightly like she knew she had me in her evil web. 'I can get Julia and Annie over here too.'

I panicked; for once my instant-excuse brain wasn't working. This was a scenario I just wasn't prepared for.

'No, don't get them. What do you want?'

She laughed. 'I just want to know what you're doing here.'

'No you don't. You want something.'

'Fair cop. There is something you can help me with.' Here it comes. 'I want to be prom queen.'

'You can't!' I spat out. 'It's a vote. I can't magic it out of the air for you.'

'Well, you magicked yourself here. I'm sure you can do it if you really think about it.'

'What if I say no?'

'Then I'll tell the school that you're imposters. That you've tricked Annie and Julia into thinking you're on the exchange. You might get arrested for being total frauds and cheating your way into innocent people's houses. I wouldn't be surprised if you just want to steal all the prom money!'

'No we don't! And you can't be arrested for being invited to somebody's house!'

'But you weren't invited. You lied and pretended you were from the exchange school. Who would do such a thing? It's all completely wrong to me. I'm sure everyone else would think so too.'

I hesitated. I believed her. We might get arrested, or at least interrogated. I was frightened!

'However,' Dawn said in a sickly sweet voice, 'if you make me prom queen I won't tell a soul. Will zip my mouth and throw away the key and let you go on your merry way.' And she mimed zipping her lips and tossing the key away.

'How would we fake you being prom queen? Because there's no way you'll get voted. You're up against Fifth Formers. How did you even get a nomination?'

She tapped the side of her nose and winked. 'That, you will never know. Let's just say it was your own fault for putting me in charge of the voting boxes. You've got till the end of the day to decide if you're going to do it. I guess you'll have to have a pow-wow with your little mate and work out a plan.'

'Why do you want to be prom queen?' I asked her. Though I probably knew the answer.

'Who wouldn't want to be prom queen?' And she wandered off to her fielding pitch giving me a parting wave as if I was her best friend.

'Tell me you're joking?' Izzy pleaded when I told her what Dawn had threatened me with on the rounders field. 'Why didn't you think up a whacky story to trick her?'

'I'm sorry, but I couldn't think of anything. I would have liked to see you try and come up with something to fob her off with,' I said crossly. Izzy sighed and picked up the rounders bibs from the grass where the kids had dropped them. We were on clear-up duty. Dawn had given us about half an hour to agree to her demands. My mind was frozen like a duff computer screen—I needed to switch it off and on again.

'I don't know how we can get round this and cheat. The votes go in the ballot box the minute the kids come through the door and hand them in. They will have ticked their choices beforehand at home.' Izzy sounded frantic.

'I know,' I answered flatly. 'Look, how about we just say yes, and tell her we'll work out how later? It doesn't really matter because we can just grab the tiara and go before they even announce the winner. Dawn will never know and when she tells everyone, we'll be long gone.'

'So, ladies, have you got an answer for me?' Dawn asked, waiting behind the bike sheds at the end of the day.

'We'll do it, make you prom queen,' I replied in a monotone.

'How?'

'We haven't worked out that bit yet.'

'Well, you better tell me soon or I'll be talking . . .'

'We'll have a plan by Friday morning, I promise,' I sighed.

'Good! Now, how's my outfit coming along?'

'So you'll leave us alone now?' I said ignoring her remark. 'That's your part of the deal.'

'Yes, yes, my lips are sealed. I've forgotten everything, unless of course you aren't successful, then I'm gonna spill those beans and watch you girls get into serious trouble!'

'How do we know you won't do that anyway?' Izzy asked suspiciously, quite rightly not believing her at all.

'You'll just have to trust me!' she had the cheek to say and laughed. 'Anyway, where are you girls from, if you're not from the International School? Are you on the run or something? Have you committed a deadly crime somewhere else?'

'We're from outer space,' I shot back.

'Yeah, sure you are. Well, I must dash.' And she disappeared off, leaving us with a bad taste in our mouths.

'What if she blabs before the prom?' Izzy said

sounding slightly hysterical. 'They might call the police. Why don't we just go home now?'

'We can't. We have to make sure our mums become friends. Julia said so herself back in the future: that they both realized that they were going to be best friends when they were dancing to Jonny's band at the prom. What if we leave and they cancel the prom to try and find us? We can't risk anything stopping the prom from happening. It totally has to go ahead.'

'Yes, you're right.' Izzy looked anguished.

'Look, don't worry. I'm sure we'll still exist at home and everything will be OK.' I patted her arm, but she shrugged it off.

'Come on, let's go. I don't want to think about it.' And she gave me a weak smile. I could tell she was thinking about it though. Once more I wondered what would happen when we did get back home. My first thought was obviously Mum being there, but after everything we'd been through in the last two weeks I wanted Izzy to still be there too. I couldn't imagine going back and not being able to talk to her about it because we were in different friendship groups. I wondered if she felt the same. Did she want to hang out like we used to? I followed her to the gates where the mums were waiting, both their heads bent over Julia's notebook.

'Hey,' I called. They both looked up.

'Check this out,' Annie said sounding really pleased. 'It's the design Julia's done for the queen's necklace.' Julia showed us.

'Wow, Julia, it's fantastic!' Izzy said proudly. It consisted of three tiers of silver and gold beads with tear-drop beads hanging down every few centimetres.

'I'm going to make it tonight. Would you help me, Izzy? I'm going to need another pair of hands to thread all these on or I'll be up all night.'

'Of course I'll help. Just show me what to do.'

'I know,' Annie proposed, 'before we go home, why don't we go and get ice cream. It's hot and we deserve it. We've all worked so hard this week.'

'What about Dawn?' Julia asked in a worried tone.

'She's not here, is she?' Annie said. 'Anyway, we're the ones who've done all the hard work.' I realized as we walked off from school, arms linked, that it wouldn't be just me who would love it when Mum came home. Dad, Nana, Julia, and Uncle Jonny would also have her there; being a wife, a friend, a daughter, and a sister as well as being my mum.

Chapter Fifteen
One More Night

Thursday mid-morning and I closed the loo cubical door and slumped on the seat. I didn't need to pee; I just needed a quiet break from painting to think. How were we going to con Dawn into believing we had a water-tight plan of deception? There was only one more day to go until Prom and Izzy and I had still drawn a blank. I looked up, Dawn's smarmy photocopied face smiled down at me. I gasped. She was everywhere! I got up—this wasn't helping. *Vote Dawn for Prom Queen!* Her home-made posters had sprung up everywhere overnight, like some kind of super mutating fungus. No one else had posters up so quickly. No one else knew they were going to get nominated . . .

'Well, ladies, I have to agree,' Miss Avery clapped her hands together at the end of the day, 'you have totally soared above all expectations. Well done on finishing on the dot. I think this prom is going to be the best thing Sir Walter Raleigh has seen for a long time. People will be talking about this in years to come.' She smiled at us all in turn.

When we got in, Nana was home from work early and there was music blasting from the kitchen.

'Mum!' Annie cried above the music, 'what's going on?' There were red and white balloons tied up everywhere on cupboards and on door handles. The table was pulled into the centre of the room, with another smaller table rammed on the end for added length, and was draped with a pure white tablecloth. In the middle a plastic Union Jack and the French flag, the Tricolour, were propped up in a crystal vase amongst some deep red velvety roses. The table was set for ten people with red paper napkins, candles, and nice glasses. It looked magical, and the smell emanating from the enormous steel pot on the stove was delicious.

'Oh, girls, you're home!' Nana turned down the music. 'Now, could someone start peeling potatoes. I'm running out of time to get everything in the oven.'

'Why, what's this?' Annie asked looking as confused as I felt.

'A goodbye party!' Nana cried spreading her arms wide and smiling. 'You didn't think Daisy was just going to slope off back to Paris and forget all about us, did you?

161

We needed to give her and Izzy a good old-fashioned British send-off!'

'Oh, Mum! What an ace idea!' Annie cried excitedly.

'Izzy, Julia, her little sister Rachel, and her parents are coming too,' Nana explained. 'Jonny's just gone round there to get some extra chairs.' I was stunned. I knew this was the second to last day, but with all the prom prep and stress with Dawn, I was kind of ignoring it. I didn't want it to be almost over. But it had to be. I felt a lump in my throat appear from nowhere. Oh, Nana, you're always so amazing.

'Wow, what's for dinner?' Izzy cried as she breezed through the door with Julia and her family later on that evening. 'We've been told there's a party. Is that true?'

'Oui, oui. French onion soup to start with,' Nana replied taking the lid off the cauldron-like pan on the hob and giving it a good stir. 'Mmm, smells good! And roast beef for the main. A Franglais dinner! I think Julia's mum is going to put together her pavlova for pudding.'

'I'm so glad I did the exchange,' Julia admitted boldly as we slurped our way through the deliciously tasty onion soup. 'You know Mum forced me, told me it would be good for me.'

'I think your mum was right,' Izzy agreed.

'Yes. At the time I thought Mum didn't have a clue, but she was just trying to help.'

'Do you think they remember being young?' Annie questioned. 'I mean, it must seem like a million years ago to them.'

I half turned to Izzy and looked at her. She smiled knowingly.

'I think they remember just fine,' she stated. 'My mum *always* says that it seems like only yesterday when she was at school and knows how I feel about stuff. Maybe she really does know.'

'Mums rock,' I said and peeked at Annie. She winked at me and grinned.

'Uh-oh, Dad's up to something!' she gasped.

Grandpa tapped his knife on his empty glass, grabbing everyone's attention.

'I would just like to say something. Two weeks ago we thought we were going to be having two American girls staying with our families for this exchange. When you two lost English roses turned up instead we were a bit surprised.' He cleared his throat. 'I know I speak for both families when I say, I am glad there was a mix-up, and we got Izzy and Daisy instead. You have both been rays of sunshine and made so much effort to join in family life. And your brilliant idea for the prom has become the talk of the school. I have seen how hard you've all worked towards this and it makes all of us very proud.' Everyone started clapping and cheering, with Uncle Jonny making the most noise by whistling loudly.

'Go, girls!' he shouted. I could feel my face burning with pride and happiness. Annie squeezed my hand. I turned and looked at her and she had tears in her eyes. I instinctively hugged her, never wanting to let go. I didn't care if I was being stalkery now. She *had* to be there when I got home—I now couldn't imagine it any other way. There wouldn't be any other way if I stuck to my plan and warned her tomorrow morning.

'I'm going to miss you guys so much,' she said, her wobbly voice muffled by my hair. 'This has been the best two weeks ever.' I pulled away and all of us linked arms and squeezed them together tightly.

'Yes, me too,' Julia agreed sounding very flat. 'I don't want you to go home. I don't know what I'll do after the prom.'

'You'll have to hang out with me!' Annie said matter of factly.

Julia smiled, a really genuinely happy smile, and I saw the Julia I know flicker across her face. Things were changing. It was all going to work out OK, I just knew it. Izzy squeezed my hand so tightly I thought she was going to crush my bones.

'I would like to finish with wishing you both well for the following year. Keep in touch!' More clapping. Julia was hugging Izzy. I wished I could record it to keep forever, so I looked round at everyone in turn and tried so hard to burn it all into my brain. Uncle Jonny winked at me and I smiled. You, Uncle, were going to get a visit as soon as I was back!

Saying goodbye late that evening, Izzy caught me before we left the kitchen.

'Hey, you OK?' I nodded. 'That was quite emotional.'

'Yes, I wasn't expecting any of that.'

'No, me neither.'

'Listen, I think I may have an idea we can feed Dawn to make her think we're going to make her prom queen.'

'Brilliant. Well done.'

'Izzy, we're going!' Julia called from the front door.

'Look, tell me tomorrow on the way to school.'

'OK, see you then.' I waved them off.

'Hey, Daisy, would you come and check over the playlist with me?' Uncle Jonny asked from the living room. 'I want to make sure you're happy with it.'

'Sure.' I scanned the piece of paper he retrieved

from his beaten up school bag. 'It looks great, good to see "Summer of 69" is on there.'

'Are you happy with it?' he asked anxiously. I had no idea what any of the songs were.

'Of course! It's amazing. You guys are going to rock the house.'

He laughed. 'You know, for a kid, you're kinda cool.' And he cuffed me on the top of my arm with his fist. I took it as a massive compliment.

'Thanks.' He grinned, his dimples upstaging his perfectly straight white teeth. I was overwhelmed by the urge to tell him not to be a recluse when he grew up.

'Listen, Jonny, a word of er . . . advice.' He raised his eyebrows in amusement. 'If you get famous, don't forget all these guys will you?'

'What? Why would I do that?'

'I don't know; I'm just saying, OK? Rock stars can go all weird and big-headed.'

'All right, Yoda! I promise not to forget my family, and to always wear a seatbelt!' He started laughing at that one. 'Now go to bed before you turn into a pumpkin!' I headed for the stairs. 'I'd better be famous!' he shouted after me.

By the time I got upstairs, Annie was in bed and looked like she was asleep—it was very late after all.

The little bedside light was still on and I sat on my camp bed and watched her while she slept. This was my last night sharing a room with my mum. I took a deep breath. Should I wake her now and have the conversation instead of in the morning? I reached over and touched her shoulder. What did it matter if we did it now or in the morning? I gently shook her and she mumbled.

'Annie,' I whispered. 'Can we talk?' My heart was pounding in my ears.

'Mmmm, Mum, is that you?' She was so drowsy.

'No, it's Daisy.'

'I was just having a dream about you.' Her eyes were still closed and she sounded half asleep.

'You were?'

'Yeah, you lived round the corner and we were best friends. It was so cool.'

'Anything else?'

'You told me you felt you'd always known me. Then I woke up. I want to go back to the dream because we were going on holiday to Spain.' She yawned. 'I do feel like I've always known you. We'll always be friends, won't we?'

'Yes,' I whispered. 'Go back to sleep.'

She dived back into her dream. I could wait one

more night and stick to the plan by telling her in the morning. I picked Pooh up and gave him a kiss.

But I couldn't sleep. Anxious about Annie's reaction, Dawn sounding off before we escaped, and just general excitement about the rest of my life being so drastically different after tomorrow, I tossed and turned for what felt like the entire night, my legs twitching so much it was like I was running in bed.

I woke with a total jump. I could hear the shower going and Annie was nowhere to be seen. I ran downstairs and Nana was having tea with wet hair waiting for the toaster to ping.

'We all overslept!' she gasped. 'Annie's just in the shower. I'm going to have to run you all to school.'

'What about Julia and Izzy?'

'Oh they've gone on without you.'

Argh! I should've told Annie last night like I wanted to! And I also needed to find out what Izzy's plan was.

Nana dropped Annie, Jonny, and I at the school gates just as Izzy and Julia rocked up.

'Do you need any help?' Izzy offered as we scrambled out of the car with the outfits for the king and queen. I handed her a bag of stuff and as I straightened up, spotted Dawn waiting ominously at the gate. While Julia and Annie ploughed on through the throng of kids, she beckoned Izzy and me to the side.

'So, what's the plan for tonight, girls?' she asked in a voice like we were her friends and this was all OK and not evil deception on a massive scale.

I looked at Izzy, hoping her plan would be enough to fool Dawn.

'Well, we thought that we could go and photocopy some fake tickets on the art room photocopier and then fill them in with you as the winner.'

'Yes, but what about the other people who won't have voted for me?'

'We take all those out of the box and replace them with your ones.'

'You reckon you can get past Miss Avery?'

'Yes—we'll carry the boxes off when everyone has arrived and swap it all over then.'

'Wow, you're good.' She looked surprised. 'See you later, ladies in waiting!'

'Argh, I wish she would get sucked into a black hole!' I grumbled once she'd disappeared.

'Yeah, well, not much longer now.'

'Good plan by the way.'

'Thanks. Right, let's get this prom on the road!'

Straight after registration, we headed down to the art

studio, where Jonny was waiting for us with Gary, one of his band mates.

'Hello, Jonny!' Dawn cried enthusiastically. 'Thanks for helping us.'

'Hi, guys,' he said to no one in particular. 'Tell me what needs carrying.'

For the next hour we shuffled giant trees, flowers, the thrones, and various other bits and bobs over to the hall. The caretaker had cleaned it all out, packing away most of the chairs and leaving some for us to scatter round the edge for kids to sit on. Jonny and Gary hefted the equipment in from a van outside—so many leads and cables—the stage had started to resemble a music festival arena on TV. I'd never ever seen Uncle Jonny's band play and had no idea what they were like. In the fabled story told to us by Julia, they were amazing. I just hoped they lived up to the hype.

'Girls, can we start arranging our equipment now, and then you lot come and do your stuff after?' Jonny called down from the stage. We were busy setting up lunch tables down one side for the hotdog stand.

'Sure thing,' I shouted back. I was watching Dawn; she kept stealing glances at Jonny. There was no clearer proof now that her drive for being prom queen was to win over Jonny. What planet was she on? Girls our age were like kindergarten kids to him! He could have the pick of the school, he wasn't going to choose a Second Year, no matter how pretty they were. It was the law of the jungle!

Dawn caught me staring and moseyed over. 'So, you better go and get photocopying in a bit, hadn't you?' I bit my lip so I didn't say anything to rile her. 'I can't wait to wear your precious tiara. Where is it? I want to try it on.'

'I left it at home. To keep it safe.'

'Well, I'll be wearing it later whether you like it or not.' I smiled at her, clenching my teeth until my jaw hurt.

'OK, people,' Jonny's voice boomed out surrounded by hideous feedback. 'We're just going to test everything now.' The rest of the band had left lessons and were milling around on the stage. 'Cover your ears if it gets too loud!'

Miss Avery turned up just then with free refreshments.

'Tea all round, and a plate of doughnuts for you girls, and one for the band.' She signalled me. 'Here, Daisy, would you take these up there to the boys?'

'No probs.' I balanced the teas on the tray with the doughnuts in the middle to even out the weight distribution. On stage I had to pick my way carefully over the wires. And just as I was doing so, Jonny blasted out some ear-bleeding chords on his guitar, making me jump. I tripped on one of the leads which wasn't yet secured with gaffer tape and the tray went flying. Five teas and a hailstorm of doughnuts spectacularly crashed down into a giant black box with loads of wires leading into it. The whole thing exploded causing a frightening bang. All the lights flicked off in the hall and the music was killed instantly. What had I done?

Chapter Sixteen
Don't You Forget About Me

Jonny carefully put down his guitar and jumped over wires and plugs to get to me.

'What were you thinking bringing tea up onto the stage?' he raged, his eyes practically popping out. 'We haven't taped everything down yet!'

'I, er, didn't know. Miss Avery asked me to bring these up to you as a treat. Then you made me jump with the guitar.'

'I didn't see you come up.'

Tears filled my eyes and spilled over onto my cheeks. I was still holding the tray, but there was nothing left on it. The plate was smashed all over the stage.

'I'm sorry,' I managed to squeak out between sobs. 'I didn't mean to.'

'Oh, Daisy, I'm sure they can fix it. Can't you?' Annie asked from the floor.

Just then one of the hall doors burst open and Mr Jimpson hurtled in.

'What's happened? All the power's gone down in the entire school.'

'There's been an accident,' Miss Avery started to explain.

'I can see that from the smoke!' Mr Jimpson bellowed. One of the other doors opened and Mr Wakely, the caretaker, strode into the hall. It was like something from a very bad comedy double-act.

'What socket have you overloaded?' he boomed to the boys and ran up onto the stage. 'Oh . . . you've blown the amp.'

'It's water damage. It's irreparable,' Jonny said in a strangled voice. I felt wretched. I'd ruined everything.

'Can you get the power back on?' Mr Jimpson asked the caretaker. 'I have to have it back on within fifteen minutes or the whole school will have to go home.'

'Yes, yes. A fuse will have blown; I'll sort it. It's all down in the basement.'

While the caretaker set off on his mission, I stood there like a lemon, wiping my eyes.

'Can I do anything?' I asked woefully. 'This is all my fault.'

Jonny shook his head having calmed down. 'The amp's totally scuppered. We need it for tonight or you guys won't hear anything.'

Mr Jimpson was now up on the stage surveying the damage.

'Right, lads, how easily can you get a new amp?'

'Not that easily,' Jonny admitted. 'We saved up for ages for this one. It cost a bomb.'

'That's not what I meant. This was an accident that happened on school grounds. I can get you a new amp. How quickly can you find one?' Jonny looked at Mr Jimpson like he was joking. 'We haven't got all day, Jonathon. Where do you go to buy one?'

'Well, I er, we got this one from the small ads in the paper, but there's a music shop in the square in town.'

'I'll go and get the Yellow Pages,' Miss Avery piped up from the floor below.

I started clearing up the spilled paper teacups, soggy doughnuts, and broken bits of plate. Annie came up and helped me.

'It wasn't your fault,' she whispered kindly as she shovelled the detritus onto the tray. 'It was an accident. Miss Avery shouldn't have asked you to come up here with tea.' I shrugged. It didn't matter. *I* had been the one carrying the tray.

'Look,' Jonny said as I made my way back down to the floor. I turned round. 'I'm sorry I shouted at you. I realize it was an accident. You didn't do it on purpose.'

'But it's messed everything up. What if you can't get an amp?'

'We'll be able to. Don't stress.'

Mr Wakely made a reappearance. 'There's good news and bad news.' I half expected him to tap dance out the answer while Mr Jimpson deadpanned it with jazz hands.

'Good news first, please,' Mr Jimpson asked with a stony face.

'I've got the power back on in the main part of the school, so no one needs to go home.'

'And the bad news?' Jazz hands.

'I forgot that the hall and the office and surrounding area are on a different circuit to the rest of the school, and the fuse board for this bit is really old and rickety—something's burnt out big time and I can't get it back on. We need an electrician to come out and sort it for us. For now there's no power in the hall.'

I wanted to cry again. How was this happening? The prom *had* to go ahead.

Half an hour later, Miss Avery was issuing instructions and people were running this way and that.

'Now, the ladies in the office are trying to locate an amp. Meanwhile, we need to act like the prom is still going ahead—we have to be prepared. So, Jonny, tape down what you can, get everything how you want it, and then the girls can come up and dress the stage.'

As we waited backstage wringing our hands, Dawn pulled me to one side.

'Don't think because you sabotaged the prom that I'm going to let you off. If this prom doesn't go ahead, I'm telling the whole world about you.' And she stormed off to the top of the steps to sit down.

'What did she want?' Izzy asked, all concerned. 'Are you OK?'

'No! I can't believe this is all happening.'

'It's going to be OK. We've got this far, haven't we?'

'But what if the prom doesn't go ahead?' I could feel panic taking over.

'Then we face that when it happens for definite.' I looked at Izzy and had a total flashback to my birthday party when I was eight. The magician didn't turn up—car trouble. I'd sat on my bed and cried. Dad had tried to cheer me up, but I wouldn't come down from my room. Izzy came up and persuaded me. 'Your dad said he will set up the Wii and we can have a dance party.'

'But that's not what I told everyone,' I'd wailed. 'They'll think it's rubbish.'

'But we all love dancing. Come on—I'll let you beat me in the dance-off.'

She'd held my hand and brought me downstairs, and now I remember that party as being the best party ever. Izzy always managed to make things OK. How had we drifted so far?

'You always know when to say the right things.'

'Not always.' Izzy looked at her hands.

'Who does?'

She shrugged. 'Listen,' I said suddenly feeling self-conscious, 'I don't want to go back to normal when we get home. It won't be *normal* when we get back.'

'What do you mean?'

'We should hang out again. You know, we need to, or what happened here will feel like it never happened . . . I miss you.' Izzy was silent and I suddenly felt like maybe I'd misjudged everything.

'I'd love to,' she said eventually.

'Phew, I thought you were going to tell me to jump off a cliff!'

'I was going to, but the frame of mind you were in I thought you might actually do it!'

'Yeah, ha ha.' Celia suddenly popped into my head. I hadn't thought about her all that much since we'd been here. It was going to be weird being friends with both her and Izzy. 'Izzy?'

'Yep?'

'What was it that Celia said to you to make you hate her?'

'I don't hate her. She's not worth me wasting the energy.'

'Well, whatever, what was it?' Izzy bit her lip and sighed.

'When I said no to her about copying my homework, she said that the only reason you were friends with me, why anyone was friends with me, was that I made them look good.'

'What does that mean?'

'She said I was so square and boring that anyone hanging out with me would automatically seem more interesting and pretty because I was the complete opposite.'

'She really said that?' Izzy nodded. 'All because you wouldn't let her copy homework?'

'Yes, I guess no one says no to her usually.'

'Why did you never tell me?'

'Because I knew you liked her and she would deny it and there seemed no point. You needed to find out for yourself what she was really like.'

'She was never ever like that to me.'

'That's because *you* made *her* look good. You're trendy and pretty and creative. She wanted you in her gang.'

I felt so awful. How could I not have realized any of this? Because you wanted to be in her gang too, a small voice said at the back of my head. I felt ashamed of not going to Izzy's party. I felt ashamed of letting us drift. Izzy had tried to stay friends and I had let it go.

'I'm sorry, Izzy. I—'

'Girls—set the stage!' Jonny suddenly announced, interrupting our chat. We jumped into action.

'It looks amazing!' Izzy breathed as we stood back and admired our handiwork a few hours later. 'I especially like the paper flowers—they look like something from a jungle. And the Christmas decos above the stage are so pretty. You're so clever, Julia.'

'I like the Chinese lanterns I bought in China Town,' Julia admitted. 'If it all works later, the fairy lights round the trees will look magical.'

'Apparently the office have found an amp in a shop in Esher, about half an hour away,' Jonny confided in us. 'It sounds like the business—better than that old heap of junk we had. Mrs James said she would go out in the school minibus and pick it up!'

'But that doesn't mean anything if the electrician can't fix the fuse board,' Gary said despondently.

'Well, we have to keep our fingers crossed,' Miss Avery tried to cheer us up. 'He's working on it now. He's said he'll try his hardest to get it done in time. But we won't know yet.' It was almost the end of school.

'We're not going to have time for a sound check,' Jonny said worriedly. 'Let's just hope everything works. Or we're going to have to listen to Mr Sheppard's tunes after all.'

'I think the best thing is, you guys go home. Have some dinner and come back in your finery just before the start time,' Miss Avery suggested.

'What if it doesn't get fixed?' I asked fearfully, knowing Dawn would out us right away.

'We'll just have to turn everyone away.'

'We need to have the tiara at the ready if the electricity is still down,' I explained to Izzy on the walk home. 'Dawn is going to blow the whistle if the prom's cancelled. She thinks I did it on purpose to stop her being queen.'

'So we just run off and do it? What about the mums?'

'Oh bum, I know. This is all getting a bit out of control.'

'Stay calm, let's think.'

'Oh, I know, we could write them a note, not to open until after the prom?'

'What if it doesn't work—they forget to read it, it gets lost—it's too risky.'

'We can't tell them; we won't have time.'

'I think we're going to have to go with it,' Izzy

reluctantly agreed. 'It really is the only option. I can write it later before we come back here.' I nodded.

'OK. Do you think we really need to go to the PE cupboard?' I wondered. 'Does it matter where we do it?'

Izzy didn't say anything—I could tell she was thinking. 'Probably not, but if we want to go back to the exact same time that we left so no one back in the future has missed us, then we need to be in the PE cupboard. It makes sense to go back from where we started.'

'OK, yes, that sounds right.' We approached Annie's gate where she and Julia waited for us to catch up.

'Right, ladies, let's get ready,' Annie said. 'See you in a few hours!'

We had bought some fairly fashion-crime nana dresses from a charity shop and customized them. I was wearing a long red dress and had sewn in a net skirt underneath to fluff it out a bit. I'd also chopped off the arms and rammed in shoulder pads. It looked cool in a futuristic kind of way (weird cos we were in the past!). I'd stuffed the torn-off photo in my bra to take back with me and show Mum. I had to believe she would be there when I got home. Annie was wearing a green maxi dress (a shirt and long straight skirt stitched together) with a chunky brown belt hiding the join. She had cut a hole out of the back. It was unusual.

'You have to wear these,' Annie insisted—a pair of massive white hoop earrings that made me feel like my ear lobes were scraping the floor (nana earlobes—stylish!). 'Look, now we match! Do you want me to do your hair? I can put some gel in it to make it all spiky?'

'Oh, thanks, that would be great.' This was it—my chance to hopefully change everything. I wiped my palms down my dress to try and soak up some of the sweat pouring out of them. Niagara Falls also seemed to be exploding from my armpits. At this rate I would need the hairdryer to blast my pits. *Please listen, Mum . . .*

'Annie?'

'Yes? Hang on; can you just stick your hair upside down while I blow-dry it? I can do your make up too?' I nodded eagerly, hiding my frazzled nerves.

'Do you believe in dreams coming true?' I finally asked when she'd finished with the hairdryer. I could barely get the words out my mouth was so dry.

'What like? Wishing something would happen and then it does?'

'No, more like you have a dream at night, when you're asleep, and then it actually happens.'

'I don't know. Do you? Close your eyes, I'm going to spray you now.'

'I do, yes.' The hairspray made me sneeze.

'Well, maybe you're right. One year I dreamt I was going to get a Girls' World for Christmas and I actually did. Does that count?'

'I think so.' But what I was going to say wasn't as fluffy as getting a Girls' World. 'You see, I've had this dream a few times since we got here. About you.'

'Oh?' She had started rummaging through her make-up bag now and was pulling out garish bright blues and greens to paint on my eyes.

'Yes, but I've dreamt about you dying in a car crash, when you're older.'

Annie stopped and looked at me. 'What? Why would you say that?'

'Because I keep having the dream. It won't go away.' I paused attempting to keep my voice normal. The hysteria was bubbling away down in the base of my belly, threatening any moment to spill over and surely render me of unsound mind in Annie's eyes. *Keep it together, Daisy.* 'What if I'm right? What if I'm here because I'm supposed to warn you, stop you from dying when you're grown up?'

Annie looked puzzled. 'But your mum died in a car crash.'

'Yes. And she wasn't careful. She dropped something on the floor of the car and undid her seatbelt to bend down to pick it up. But she crashed into another car.' That was what the verdict had been, anyway.

'I'm not your mum,' Annie said quietly. 'I think you're just having a dream because of your mum and the fact we were talking about her the other day.'

'But what if you're supposed to hear this?' I squeaked, desperation starting to creep into my voice. 'What if this stops you from dying?'

Annie shook her head. 'I'm not going to die in a car crash. I know you're worrying that it's some sort of fortune telling dream, but it isn't.'

'OK, but do you promise me that when you have a car, you won't drop your phone on the floor and try and pick it up when you're driving?'

Annie laughed. 'A phone? Why would I have a phone in my car? That's crazy!' I must have looked upset because she stopped laughing. 'Yes, I totally promise that I won't ever take my hands off the steering wheel. I will be a careful driver.'

'And wear a seatbelt?'

'Yes, I will wear a seatbelt.' She looked right at me and smiled kindly, but there was something else lurking there too: pity. 'Now can I finish doing your eyes or you're going to look weird?' I nodded. I couldn't speak because I felt so scared. I wasn't sure this was going to work. I should have just gone straight in with 'I'm your daughter', but the truth sounded properly insane and she would surely freak out at me, making everything worse.

'Here, look.' She handed me a mirror a few minutes later, snapping me out of my internal turmoil. I didn't recognize myself. She had given me massive hair and bright blue mega-cringe eyeshadow—I looked like I was in one of Mum's Eighties fashion books, and kind of pulled it off. 'Wow, I love it!' I said unexpectedly. I meant it—it was kooky and cool. I got up and pulled something out from under my bed. 'Here, I made you this.'

'Oh, ace! It's one of your bags.' I'd made it from off-cuts of the queen's outfit and some scrap material Annie had knocking around in her sewing basket. 'When did you have time to do this?'

'When you were asleep one night. I just stayed up and did it.'

'It's sooo cool. That's very sweet of you.' And she grabbed me and pulled me in for a hug. She smelled of Impulse and hairspray. I wanted to stay in the hug forever, but she drew away. 'Now, you must write down your address before you go so I can write to you. Remember—we're going to be pen pals!' I nodded. 'And don't worry about your dream—it won't come true.' *Pen pals*—I could write my first letter right now! You can't think a letter is acting crazy, or shout insults at it and make it cry. It's just a letter. It doesn't have feelings.

Dear Annie,

Please read this letter all the way to the end before you freak out. Remember when I was telling you about the dream I had of you dying? It's actually real. That happens. I am from the future. I arrived the morning of the exchange by total freak accident (one day I can explain!). I am your daughter. You died when I was four and I have a chance to save you and have you living with Dad and me forever.

I want to know what it's like to have you kiss me goodnight all the time. I want to know what it's like to have you sit with me and teach me proper pattern cutting or go to the park on our bikes or tell me what it was like being young in the Eighties or how to be strong like Nana (your mum). I want a second chance, that's all.

You were so amazing, and I barely remember it, but everyone says so. And so happy—you loved Dad so much. Even if you don't believe a word I am saying, keep this letter forever. Look at it and remember what I told you about never taking your seatbelt off. Ever. I promise you won't regret it. This is our secret—you can't tell anyone. I love you more than you will ever know. I just wish I could have told you to your face today. I miss you. Please come home.

Always yours

Daisy x

Chapter seventeen
Summer of 69

Nana dropped us all at the school, but not before we'd had to have our photo taken in the back garden. Annie had cajoled me into wearing white staggery stiletto heels. 'Look, everyone wears them. It's the law!' I laughed inside because Dad would never ever let me wear anything like that in a million years, and here Mum was forcing me to!

'Cheese,' Nana chimed.

'Cheeeeeeeeeeese.' Izzy had instructed me to move my head at the last minute so our faces would blur out.

'We can't have any evidence we were here,' she hissed in my ear as we trudged out to the garden. 'I don't want Mum noticing us in pictures back in the future.' Best not mention my letter then . . .

'Here's the note I wrote to our mums,' Izzy said taking me to one side after the photo. 'Is it OK?'

Dear Annie and Julia,

We think you two would be better
off being friends as you are both super
cool and have way more in common than
you think.
    Sorry we just disappeared without a
proper goodbye, but we had to go. We
loved meeting you and had the best time.
Thank you for looking after us. Have
amazing lives and maybe see you again
one day.

Lots of love
Daisy and Izzy xxx

I nodded.

'Can you put it in the bag with the tiara?' she said.
I dropped it in where I'd secretly stashed my letter to
Annie. I'd thought about leaving the letter on her bed,
but wanted to see for definite she'd received it. Last
minute hand delivery it was then.

As we walked quietly up to the front doors of the
school, we collectively held our breath.

'There's no power,' Annie sighed as we entered. 'Look, no lights or anything.'

'Oh, no!' Julia cried. 'Will they cancel it, do you think?'

'When I left to come back and get changed, Miss Avery said they would leave it right up until the last minute,' Jonny explained as we stood at the entrance watching the dinner ladies laying out hotdog rolls. 'Five to, she said.'

'Come on, Izzy, let's pretend to check on stuff backstage,' I whispered. Izzy was struggling to walk in Julia's borrowed ridiculous wobbly heels, so took them off. Her bright pink sundress was covered in ruffles all along the bottom and there were shoulder pads like mattresses stuffed into a matching shiny pink bolero jacket. She looked ridiculous.

'Oh, Izzy,' I giggled. 'I wish I had my phone so I could take a picture of you to show Ethan. He would die laughing.'

She glared at me. 'I didn't have a choice. It was either this pink outfit or something even worse.' What could be worse, I thought. Then Dawn rocked up. Oh, *that* was worse.

'Hello, ladies. Keep my crown safe, won't you?' She teetered on patent neon-pink stilettos, sporting a white glittery crop top and then some hideous puffball white skirt. She looked like a lollipop in reverse. The Eighties had a lot to answer for—there were so many fashion offences, someone needed to be arrested.

'It's almost quarter to,' Izzy said tensely as we clattered up the steps at the side of the stage. 'We need to be ready to run to the PE cupboard the minute Miss Avery mentions anything about cancelling. We make a dash for our mums and give them our letter.'

'Let's just wait here then until we know what's happening.' I watched Annie and Julia from where we stood hovering in the wings. If the prom were cancelled, we wouldn't get to say goodbye. I was gutted, but was certain Annie's letter would work its magic. I planned to hand it to her alongside the joint letter from Izzy and me.

Miss Avery pushed through the hall doors, no doubt to find out what the plan was. At five to, she still hadn't come back in.

'Look, the door . . .' Izzy hissed.

'I've an announcement,' Miss Avery began in a grave voice as she re-entered.

'Run!' Izzy gasped. 'Now. Get ready with the letter.' I whipped both letters out of the bag hiding my note to Annie behind the other letter. We hurtled down the stairs, leaving our shoes behind on the stage. I grasped the bag super tightly and we ran towards our mums like our lives depended on it.

'Whoa! Girls, what's the rush?' Annie cried startled.

'Here, have this!' And I thrust the envelopes at her. 'We've got to go.'

Dawn's face was furious. I thought she was going to start shouting, but it was someone else who shouted.

'Girls, come back. It's good news!' Miss Avery cried at our retreating backs. 'The power's just about to go back on.' And as if by magic, all the lights burst into life in the hall. Izzy stopped abruptly and I smacked right into her.

We turned round mortified. Dawn was laughing her head off at us. And Julia and Annie were looking totally perplexed.

'What's this?' Annie asked as we slunk back the way we had come. She was waving an envelope at us.

'And where were you going?' Julia questioned.

Think, Daisy, think! An excuse . . .

'Yes, ah, you see, we were desperate for the loo, and wanted to go before the crowds arrived. We're on the door and didn't think we'd get a chance.'

'But what's the letter?' Annie insisted.

'It's for you to open after we've left. It's a thank you letter. It's embarrassing so save for when we're not here.'

'Ah, sweet, thank you!' Annie smiled. 'Give me the tiara, I'll put it backstage—go to the loo. Everyone will be arriving now!'

I had no choice but to hand the bag over. We traipsed outside and pretended to find the toilet; instead we dodged behind a tree.

'So, what do we do now?' I asked. 'They've got the tiara.'

'We need to man the door, so Dawn thinks we're going to fake her votes,' Izzy said practically. 'Then we'll just grab the tiara when all the votes have been cast. They will need to count them all—that takes a while—and we can leave just before the announcement. Easy peasy.'

'Can people slow down?' I shouted ten minutes later to the incoming crowd. Kids were pushing trying to get in. 'Izzy, can you grab Annie and Julia? We need help. The tide of bad taste needs marshalling.' I'd never seen so many shiny suits or white stilettos in my life.

'Sure. If you lit a match I reckon the whole hall would explode, the amount of hairspray going on here,' Izzy laughed, clicking away on the tally counter.

Half an hour after kick-off and it was time for the band to go on. 'Kids are getting twitchy,' Annie pointed out as the final stragglers filtered in to the hall. 'No one will dance to the mix tape because they're waiting for Jonny. Is he ready?'

'I'll go and check,' Julia offered.

'Nearly everyone here?' Dawn asked sneaking up on me, glancing down at the tally counter in my hand.

'Almost.'

'Where're the fake tickets?'

I faltered, I never thought she would ask. 'Er, ummm . . . in the bag with the tiara.'

She bored her eyes right into mine, narrowing them. 'Really?'

'Yes!'

'Fine.' She turned on her heels and stalked off. I wondered if she was going to check.

'Annie—where did you put the tiara?' I asked her as she let the final few in.

'Backstage on the table where the costumes are.' I nodded. Suddenly Jonny's band blasted out the first chord of their opening song.

'Hello, Sir Walter Raleigh!' Jonny shouted over the mic, making it screech with feedback, so that the other guitarist leapt over to the new amp to fiddle with some knobs. Kids were covering their ears. 'Sorry about that, we're The Wild Boys, and this is your first ever prom!!!'

A wave of noise hit me, and I realized everyone was cheering like loons, their voices becoming one unified bellow. Kids were really going for it with the first tune. I had no idea what it was, some vaguely familiar Eighties rock song.

'What?' Izzy was shouting something at me. 'I can't hear you.' Jonny's band was so loud.

''Look at the counter!' she gestured to it. I looked down: four hundred. We were full. She picked up the voting box. 'It's time,' she mouthed and nodded her head towards the stage and smiled sympathetically. She knew this was going to be hard for me. Julia had joined Annie and they were watching the stage by the door, totally mesmerized. We walked over to them.

'Come outside a second!' Izzy shouted in Annie's ear. It was still loud in the corridor but the doors buffeted some of the sound, so just the bass reverberated in your chest. My ears were already tingling inside.

'We just wanted to say well done,' Izzy started. 'The prom looks amazing. We couldn't have done any of it without you.'

'I know!' Annie cried. 'I love it! It looks so professional. It looks like a wonderland.'

'I LOVED doing it all,' Julia enthused. 'Thank you for making me.'

'What's the matter, Daisy?' Annie asked, concerned. 'You look sad.'

I jumped. I hadn't realized my face was betraying me. 'Nothing. I'm OK. I just want to remember this forever.' I smiled at them both. This *wouldn't* be the last time I saw Annie. She was going to come home, I just knew it. So why were tears prickling my eyes? Why did I want to try and drag her with us to the PE cupboard?

'Well, let's get out there and party!' Annie laughed, grabbing my hand. 'It's our last night!'

'We have to take the voting box back to Miss Avery,' Izzy explained in a stiff voice. 'She's waiting to count.'

'You go,' I said to Annie reluctantly. 'Go and dance with Julia. We'll join you in a bit.'

'You sure?' she asked. I nodded, words catching in my throat, tears threatening.

'Oh, girls, we're going to miss you,' Julia said suddenly her voice wobbling slightly.

'We'll miss you too,' Izzy answered meaningfully and she uncharacteristically swept me and Julia in on Annie for a group hug.

This was finally it, I thought. Time to go. 'Girls rock!' Izzy said, her voice sounding thick with tears. 'We know how to do stuff properly. Go and show them how to dance,' she said to the mums. We pushed through the hall doors and were immediately enveloped by the heat and wall of sound. Sweat pricked in my armpits.

'See you in a bit!' Julia cried over her shoulder as she and Annie shimmied their way to the dance floor. I wiped my eyes. Goodbye, Mum, for now . . .

We tottered over to the stage steps with the box ready to hand it to Miss Avery backstage for the count.

'Look!' Izzy cried from behind me. 'They're dancing!' We stopped on the first step and watched.

Point three had finally been reached on Operation Hairspray! The mums were friends.

3. Mums MUST become BFFs ✓

They were laughing and doing some odd swirly dance, flicking their solid hair at the same time. Just then the opening mega chords of 'Summer of 69' echoed out over the bobbing sea of heads. A forest of hands shot up in the air as if to catch the notes.

'Got my first real six string . . .!' Jonny was singing like a true rock god, Annie and Julia linked hands and screamed, jumping up and down in time with the music. 'And that's when I met you!' Both of them were singing in time with Jonny and surprised us both with some serious air guitar action. The crowd was going bonkers—everyone knew every single lyric. It surely had to be the song of the night even though it was only the second song in!

'We better go,' I cried into Izzy's ear above the noise. 'I think it's safe to leave now.'

Reluctantly we turned away from the crowd, and I banged straight into Dawn.

Chapter eighteen
The Heat Is On

'Where do you think you're going?' Dawn shouted accusingly above the music.

'To give Miss Avery the box,' I cried equally loud.

'There were no fake tickets with the tiara, just a letter!' And she produced the faithful bag from behind her back and pulled out the envelope with Annie's name on it—it was the letter from me! 'You were never going to do it, were you? You were going to do a runner and tell Annie all about my plan; that's what this letter's for.'

'No, we're going to do it now!' Izzy yelled. 'Just give us the tiara.'

'No, not until you prove to me you've done it,' she snarled.

'If you give us the tiara, we'll do it,' I bargained, panic gripping my throat. I couldn't believe I'd only given Annie the letter from Izzy and I. I could have sworn I'd picked my letter up too. I'd been in such a rush. Argh!

'No.'

I lunged at the bag but she whipped it away before I could snatch it.

'Just give us the bag!' I practically screamed. She smiled and shook her head. 'No one in their right mind would EVER think you deserved to win. You're crazy! Of course we were never going to make you prom queen!'

There, I'd said it, all the things I'd wanted to say to her. She looked taken aback.

'Is that so? Well, I guess you won't be having your precious tiara then. Useless piece of junk.'

'Oh yes we will,' Izzy cried. 'It's ours!'

'Make me!' And with that she jumped back up the steps and onto the side of the stage.

'Follow her!' Izzy yelled as she kicked off her spiky-heeled shoes. I did the same and dashed up onto the stage, looking at the floor for taped-down cables. Izzy scarpered through the throngs of kids jumping around to the music at the front of the stage. She was going to block the other entry of escape on the stage—the opposite set of steps on the left. Jonny looked surprised when Dawn jumped behind him, almost tripping on his guitar lead. Then he saw me and pulled a 'What's going on?' face.

Izzy had reached the other stairs by the wings in

lightning speed without her shoes on. We had trapped her. Dawn looked frantically at me and then rushed to the front of the stage, kicking off her hideous pink shoes and jumped off into the crowd below. All the while the band kept on playing and when she jumped, the crowd cheered, obviously thinking it was part of the show. Izzy ran back down the stairs and gave chase again, pushing people out of the way. I forgot she was such a fast runner. I followed in hot pursuit, trying to see where Dawn was heading next. I watched as one of the hall doors swung open and Dawn barged through it. Izzy charged through another one with me trailing behind.

'That way!' Izzy ordered as Dawn disappeared out of the front doors by the office and into the courtyard.

Dawn was standing on the far side of the filthy green school pond. A film of icky-looking gunge slicked smoothly across the surface like a greasy skin on top of the school gravy. Dawn eased the tiara out of the bag. It sparkled in the evening sunlight blinding me so I had to shield my eyes. I knew what she was going to do and was powerless to stop her.

'If you want your darling tiara so badly, then you can go and get it.' Izzy was legging it round the edge of the pond like a sprinter on sports day. But she didn't get there in time. Dawn swung her arm over her head and chucked our way back home into the murky water. The tiara cut the disgusting gunge into fragments as it sank to the bottom. She ripped the letter to shreds and scattered the pieces like confetti onto the surface of the water.

'You cow!' Izzy raged, and shoved Dawn really hard when she reached her. Dawn wasn't expecting it and in a comedy style slow-mo tumble, she toppled into the pond, her arms windmilling to try and prevent the inevitable. Her fall caused a mini tsunami to slop over the edge and I clapped my hand to my mouth. We'd crossed all kind of lines now. As soon as her head slammed under the surface, she was jumping up, choking out the foul water.

'You evil witch! I'm so going to get you for this. Wait till everyone knows you're complete liars.' Izzy stood her ground. And stared her down as Dawn slipped trying to get out. By this time I'd jogged round to meet Izzy. The letter was too shredded to rescue.

'We're not scared of you,' Izzy growled dangerously. 'Girls like you are cowards inside. Go on, run along; go tell the teacher on us. DO IT!' she screamed like a crazy loon, making me jump out of my skin. For the first time Dawn looked frightened. *I* was frightened—I'd never seen Izzy lose it like that before. Her eyes were bulging and she was shaking.

'Who are you people?' Dawn whispered, shivering as her wet clothes suctioned themselves to her body. She backed away like *we* were the nasty pieces of work and ran inside leaving a splattering trail of pond water.

'We've got to get that tiara now,' Izzy said, switching from scary psycho to normal Izzy in a flash. 'She'll be in there in no time blabbing—we've got to go!'

'OK, come on then.' I grabbed her hand and we sloshed into the pond together.

'Come on, it went in over here. Was it a letter to your mum?' I nodded.

'You OK?'

I shook my head.

'I totally get why you wrote it, I really do, but the minute we find the tiara, we're legging it to the gym. No last minute revelations to Annie—there's no time. The future has to be what it will be.'

I looked at her and she smiled sadly. I squeezed her hand.

Oh, Mum, please remember what I said about the seatbelt . . .

We waded over to the place where the oil slick of grossness had separated.

'That's my foot!' I cried as Izzy tried to yank it up from the bottom. We patted around hopelessly along the spongy pond bed like players in blind man's buff.

I grabbed something and brought out a pencil case covered in algae, chucking it back immediately. 'Here, I think this is it.' I felt something sharp and grasped it. Like Arthur retrieving the fabled sword from the stone, I drew out the tiara from its watery grave. 'Ta da!'

'Well done! Now let's get out of here!' We slithered our way back to the side and stepped out. 'We smell.' I nodded; a whiff of mouldy slime wafted up my nostrils.

'You were . . . amazing with Dawn,' I said to Izzy, full of admiration.

'It was a long time coming.' She shrugged. 'She's probably blabbing right now, but the quickest way to the gym by far is straight back through the hall and out by the hotdog stall. If we go in right at the back of the dancing no one will spot us. There're four hundred kids! It's the last place anyone would look for us.'

'Yes, you're right. Let's go then.'

Operation Hairspray was finally complete.

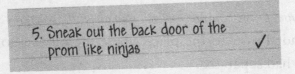

5. Sneak out the back door of the
   prom like ninjas ✓

Tiara in hand we dashed back into school. The music was still blasting out of the hall as we slipped sneakily in the furthest door from the stage. And that's when I made the mistake of looking up at the stage instead of concentrating on trying to get to the exit. Dawn stood on the stage to the right waving her hands around to Miss Avery who was pulling a disbelieving face. Annie and Julia were standing next to her their faces looking pinched in concentration. Dawn spotted me right at that moment, catching my eye, her mouth dropping open. Oh, scrap point five—that was never going to get ticked off now!

'Run!' I shouted at Izzy. 'They've seen us!' But we had to contend with barging through a gyrating tightly-knit crowd of kids who didn't want to get out of the way.

'Oi, stop it!' 'You smell, ewwww!' 'Go the other way.' We were only halfway through when Dawn and Miss Avery, followed by Julia and Annie, attempted to follow us through the wall of kids.

'She's going to be sick!' Izzy screamed. 'Out of the way! She's going to vom, any second. Mind, mind!' I covered up my mouth like I was going to puke everywhere and like magic, the kids parted, terrified of being splattered by chunks of carrot. This revealed the fire escape directly in front of me with the hotdog stand to the right. There were huge notices plastered all over it saying to only use it in an emergency. This seemed like one to me. I pushed the door—it didn't budge.

'Harder!' Izzy shouted. 'They'll be here any second.' I shoved it; it remained closed. 'Press the bar down!' I duly did that and the door swung open and immediately the fire alarm exploded above my head. Kids started shrieking and Jonny's band stopped instantly. Dawn had reached the edge of the crowd. Izzy turned round and with the reflexes of a ninja, grabbed the small hotdog oven next to the door and tipped it over onto its side across the doorway, hotdogs and hotdog juice spilling everywhere over the floor and into the crowd beyond. 'Free hotdogs!' she cried as total chaos ensued.

'To the gym!' she yelled like a sergeant ordering troops into battle.

My bare feet hurt like hell on the paved ground. Izzy reached the gym door before me. She slammed her body into it she was running so fast, like a cartoon character leaving a body-shaped hole where they never stopped. She grabbed the door handle and yanked it.

'It's locked!' she wailed.

'Let me try!' It was shut fast. 'Quick, down the side, they're gonna be here in a minute.' There was a small alleyway to the right between the back of the canteen where the bins were. Izzy ran to the end.

'Bingo! Two windows!' She pointed up at the wall above.

'Of course, the changing rooms!' I cried gleefully. 'Brilliant! We just have to get up there.' They were really high up the wall, much taller than we were. A ladder was needed.

'The bins!' I shouted, grateful my brain was still in gear. 'Come on.' They were a bit further back down the alleyway and surprisingly light and I picked one up quite easily on my own and carried/dragged it to the spot below one of the windows. 'I'm much taller than you, so maybe I should go first?' Izzy nodded frantically.

'The window's open a tiny bit!' I cried joyfully. But try as I might I couldn't budge it. That was when I realized it was fixed on a hook on the inside.

'What's wrong?' Izzy hissed.

'I need to unhook it.' I reached my fingers in the gap and grazed the hook, unable to touch it properly.

'Hurry!' Izzy urged.

I tried again, this time managing to push the hook halfway out of the eye it was resting in.

'They're coming!' Izzy panicked down below. 'I can hear them.'

One more shove and the hook popped out and I pulled the window towards me. I was able to grab the inside of the ledge and haul myself up. The fear was bubbling away at the base of my throat. I heaved my stomach over the ledge and looked down into the murky darkness below. 'DO it,' I said to myself. I dived over the edge and crashed down onto a bench, managing to avoid bashing my head.

'Daisy? *Daisy*? Are you OK?' Izzy's concerned voice cried through the window.

'Yes, get on the bin and climb through!' I yelled. 'I can catch you.'

'I can't reach the window ledge. I'm too short!' she screamed. 'Dawn's seen me!'

I looked wildly round the room. A bank of empty lockers stood next to the window. I slammed my shoulders against them. They rocked once, but resolutely rested back in place. I tried again with more force and as they rocked this time, I grabbed the top of them and pulled with all my might. They came crashing down on the bench. I pushed the bench out of the way so they could lie flat. I hopped up and was now able to reach over the window ledge.

'Pass me the tiara then grab my arms!' I screamed at Izzy as Dawn shouted from the alley entrance.

'They're here!' she yelled to the entourage.

I grabbed the tiara and placed it gingerly on the

lockers. I then hung out of the window and clasped
Izzy's arms and started dragging her up the wall as she
tried to get a grip on the bricks with her bare feet. I
managed to get my hands under her armpits and stepped
back a bit to find some space to pull her through and
she collapsed onto the lockers.

'I think she'll come through the window if she can,'
Izzy said urgently.

Silently we ran to the corridor outside, through the
gym hall door, sprinting as fast as we could to the blue
PE cupboard door.

She opened it and we peered into the darkness
beyond. She stepped in before me and groped around
for the light switch.

'Don't do that. She'll see where we are!' I cried.
Just then I heard a crash. That must have been Dawn
colliding with the lockers in the changing room.

'The lights were on when we arrived,' Izzy snapped.
'They need to be on again. It has to be the same.'

Shutting the door behind us, we both clambered
over the mats to the gap at the back by the net bag of
footballs.

'Put it on,' Izzy squeaked. 'HURRY!'

I jammed the tiara on my head, my hands wobbling.
'Now what?' I asked in a panic.

'Ask to go home. Really want it.'

'Please can I go back home? I just want to see my dad and Nana again, and my mum. I want my family back together again.' I never wanted anything so much in my entire life. I shakily handed Izzy the tiara—it was glowing and then started fizzing like a light bulb about to blow. The door to the gym hall slammed open. 'She's here,' I whispered feverishly, my head started to spin and I sank to my knees as a wave of nausea washed over me. I grabbed Izzy's hand like it was a lifeline.

'Please can I just go back to the exact time that we left? And please, please can I still exist? I want to see my family and friends again and just be a normal thirteen year old.' I could hear footsteps thumping up the hall towards the cupboard door. The handle twisted and the light pinged off, throwing the cupboard into total darkness.

Chapter Nineteen
Life in One Day

'Open your eyes, Izzy,' I hissed. 'Open them.' We were in the dark and someone was turning the handle of the PE cupboard door.

I felt my stomach violently dip, like I had unexpectedly jumped off the highest diving board at the pool.

'Girls, come on! What's keeping you?' Izzy let go of my hand.

'Oh!' Izzy gasped in surprise. Mrs Upton stood there in her netball skirt, silhouetted against the lights from the gym.

I didn't know how we were going to explain this. We were both still wearing massacred prom dresses, loads of make-up and hideous earrings. Our feet were damp and black and covered in cuts. We looked like escapees from a disaster movie: *The Land That Fashion Forgot*. My head was still throbbing and the nausea was overpowering. As we emerged into the light, blinking, furious whispering and some giggling exploded round the gym. Mrs Upton stared at us, dumbfounded, but soon found her voice.

'What on earth have you been doing in there?' she shouted at us. 'What are you wearing?'

I didn't know what to say. I felt like I needed to sit down and just be silent. I looked towards the crowd of kids gawping at us and caught Celia laughing. We'd been away for two weeks, but these guys had no idea.

'We found an archive box in the PE cupboard and decided to open it,' Izzy began hesitantly. Mrs Upton raised her eyebrows. 'These costumes were inside, along with some other stuff and we decided to try them on.' Thankfully Izzy had finally found her inner liar because I think I'd left my brain back in 1985.

'So you're telling me that in the few minutes you were in there, you've managed to apply all that make-up, put on those clothes, and look like you had a catfight on the floor?' I looked down at my arms—they were grazed to death. As soon as I noticed them, they started to sting. Izzy was in a similar state to me.

'Yes,' I just said rather quietly. What else could we say? Er, well, you see we tried on the tiara, and ended up travelling through a time portal in the PE cupboard to 1985 where we organized the prom, met our mums, lied to everyone about who we were, made an epic getaway, fought our way into the school PE cupboard, and made it back here where you see us standing now. Yes, *that* sounded believable!

'I think you'd better just go back to the changing rooms and get cleaned up. Wipe all that muck off your faces, please. When you're ready, sit in the corridor outside and wait for the end of the lesson.' I got the feeling she didn't really know what to do with us. There was no way we looked like we were telling the truth. How could you do all that in a few minutes and get into such a mess?

'You can't go rooting through school property like that and expect to get away with it. You'll both be getting detention.'

'Sorry, Mrs Upton,' Izzy mumbled.

'Yes, sorry,' I echoed.

'Go on, go!'

Izzy was still wearing the tiara and removed it as we sloped off towards the exit. I could hear excited gossiping and laughing behind us.

'Don't think you can make that noise!' Mrs Upton shouted. 'Alex, Liam, help me get the mats out of there!'

Once we were back in the changing rooms, the very same ones we had just escaped from, I slumped on the bench below my hung-up clothes.

'I've got a banging headache,' Izzy complained rubbing her temples.

'Me too. Did all of that really happen? I mean, I'm sitting here thinking it did, but now we're back, it seems impossible.'

'I was almost being sick with fear when Dawn spotted us. You have no idea how scary she looked. She was like a Rottweiler. I dread to think what she'd have been like if she'd actually caught us.' I shuddered.

'It was a close escape, that's for sure.'

'Yeah, I'm not keen for any of that craziness any time soon.'

'Do you think we would have been arrested?' I wondered. 'I mean, imagine if we hadn't escaped or found the tiara. Who would we say we were?'

'Tell the truth.'

'But no one would have believed us.'

'I think they would in the end. Especially when I invented the iPhone!' I laughed, but the thought of being trapped there forever did leave me feeling shaky, even if I was with Mum. Because I wouldn't see Dad . . .

'We've got to get rid of *that* tiara as soon as possible.'

'Which is funny because we spent half our time stressing about finding it!'

'It's done its job—let's drop it in a charity shop on

the way home. Let someone else have a go!' It wasn't so sparkly now. In fact it looked quite ordinary.

'I'm sorry about your letter,' Izzy said as we got dressed after showering. I shrugged. 'Did you do something else to warn her, Daisy? You must have because you asked to see your mum again in the PE cupboard.' I nodded slowly. 'You didn't say anything that would change anything, did you? Like warn her not to be a stylist or learn to drive, or tell her who we were?' I shook my head.

'I just warned her to wear a seatbelt at all times.'

'OK, that seems fairly safe—and we still exist so that's all good. It's just that the Butterfly Effect can do weird things with time. You just never ever know what, that's all.'

'I get that, but you have no idea what it was like for me being with her. You have a mum to come back to, even if you don't get on with her.'

'I know and I'm very grateful I do,' Izzy said contritely. 'One thing this trip has taught me—it's hard being a teenager whatever decade you're in! I always thought she had no idea what it felt like.'

'And you can tell her that, kind of. I've never had the chance to know what it's like to have a mum there all the time to fall out with or whatever. Now maybe I will . . .'

'Aren't you worried about the impact?' Izzy asked as she pulled on her socks. 'If she's here, I mean. What if you have a brother or sister? Or she's no longer married to your dad? Or some other strange soap opera type of fall out? It's still the Butterfly Effect, but she's alive.'

'I never thought that far ahead. I just want to see her.'

Izzy nodded. 'Let's hope it's all OK then.'

We waited outside on the benches in the corridor like Mrs Upton had asked us to. Mr Wakely, the caretaker, passed us with a giant broom.

'In trouble again, girls?' And he winked.

'Did you see that?' Izzy hissed.

'I know, do you think he knows?'

'No, how could he?' I shrugged. After what had happened in the last two weeks, anything was possible as far as I was concerned.

The clock on the wall said we had fifteen minutes until the end of the day. My stomach felt like a butterfly farm and I couldn't keep my feet still. I was ready to run.

'Look, I think I'm going to take off.'

'Now? It's not the end of lessons yet.'

'I realize that, but I have to get home. I need to see if Mum's there.'

'Yes, I would be the same. Let's go then.'

'You don't have to come. You'll get in even more trouble.'

'Daisy, I'm not letting you go on your own. We're in this together. What difference will fifteen minutes make to them? We're in mega trouble as it is. Bailing early is the least of our worries.'

I hugged her. 'Thanks!'

We gathered up our bags and pushed through the door. We ran as fast as we could through the deserted school campus until we reached the familiar front gate. I pressed the release button. A bus was just pulling up outside.

'Quick, leg it!' Izzy ordered. 'I don't think anyone saw us.'

I couldn't talk on the bus so I just stared out of the window. Everything looked just the same, but was it? We walked past Help The Aged on the route home and popped in.

'We'd like to donate this,' Izzy said, producing the tiara from its hiding place once we were at the cash desk.

The old lady looked so mesmerized that I instantly knew the tiara was never going to make it onto the shop floor.

'She's going to have the adventure of a lifetime,' I said as we left.

'Several lifetimes!'

'What if this isn't my house?' I asked waveringly, as we approached the front gate. 'What if . . . she's in there? What if everything's messed up?' My palms felt cold and clammy.

'Do you want me to come in with you?'

'No. I need to be on my own, I think. Thanks, though.'

'Shall I come round later?' Izzy asked tentatively.

I smiled. 'Yes, that would be great. I hope everything's OK at your house.'

'Me too. I'm sure it will be. Unless Mum left Dad and decided to run off with the circus while I was gone.'

'It's a possibility . . .' She laughed. 'Ooooh, this is just tooooo strange. It all is. I'm really scared . . .'

'Come here.' And she gave me a hug.

'So we tell no one about this?' Izzy asked. 'No one would believe us anyway.'

'Yep, lips sealed. I'm not sure *I* even believe it. Everything so far is like we've never been away. Maybe it never happened and we just had a massive hallucination?'

'Perhaps . . .' Izzy looked thoughtful. 'Look, there's something you should know. I did wish for something when we were in the PE cupboard.'

'Ooooh, what?'

'For us to be friends again. I missed you. Being in that cupboard and messing around reminded me of how we used to be. And I've missed that . . .'

'Then your wish came true!' I laughed, hugging her. 'We make a good team.'

'Let me know what happens, you know, with . . . your mum.' Izzy smiled and heaved her bag on her shoulder ready to go. 'Text me later—oh wow, I can say that now!!! Weird!' And she wandered off to see if everything was OK in her world.

I stood outside the gate, not sure whether to go in or not. What if . . .? I pushed the gate and stumbled up to the front door, digging around in my bag for the key. I turned the key. It still worked—phew! I stepped inside.

Chapter twenty
Too Late For Goodbyes

The clock in the hall was ticking very loudly like a metronome. Rogues' Gallery stared back at me—all those eyes following my every move. I was almost too afraid to look properly. The wedding photo was still pride of place in the centre. There was a new photo as well of a very young Mum and Dad, Julia, Dave (her husband and Izzy's dad) with Uncle Jonny, all grinning and holding up champagne glasses to the camera. Uncle Jonny was grasping what looked like a framed gold CD in the other hand. Uncle Jonny the hermit? That's weird. There was another one of him doing a cartwheel as I clapped—I looked about eight or nine. I don't remember that at all. The one of Dad and I in Spain was still up there but there were no new photos of Mum on the wall. Sobs involuntarily rumbled from the base of my belly and escaped through my mouth.

'She's not here,' I gasped, tears spurting like sprinklers from my eyes. 'She didn't listen to me.' I slid down the opposite wall like a rag doll and sat hugging my legs into me, pressing my eye sockets into my knees. I didn't know how long I sat there all scrunched up, trying to stem the endless tide of tears. 'I sh-should've left the note on her bed,' I wailed out loud. More tears, more blaming myself. Gradually the tears subsided and I unfolded my body, my limbs feeling stiff from the tense hold I'd locked them in. I stood up. I was going to look—it felt like picking a scab.

I trudged shakily up the stairs and pushed open the door to Dad's room. It looked Spartan like it always did; the dressing table housing a picture of him and Mum and me and his lone bottle of aftershave.

I pulled open the wardrobe door, just jeans and a few shirts—no dresses, no staggeringly high heels, no fancy outfits. There were no more tears—I just felt numb. I didn't know if I would be able to feel anything ever again.

I wandered down the stairs and into the kitchen, not really knowing what to do with myself. I looked wildly around and spotted a giant white cake box sitting on the oven hob surrounded by bags of posh crisps. Look in it, do it! the voice in my head said. So I gingerly opened the flimsy cardboard lid to reveal an enormous white cake. And on the cake was piped the words in gold icing:

Congratulations on your engagement, with gold hearts scattered across the top. I thought I was going to vom there and then, all over the pristine cake—I didn't think things could get any worse. I fell back against the kitchen table behind me. My head exploded and the nausea that half-heartedly threatened now overwhelmed me so I had rush to the sink and heave into it. Nothing came out, just gasps and choking. How could things have changed so much? How was Dad getting married so soon? Maybe it wasn't soon. Maybe in the new future, because of something I did in 1985, he'd met Mary much, much earlier. I racked my brains to think of anything we had done that could have caused this disaster. I ran into the hall to check the pictures again and smashed right into Dad. I hadn't heard the door because I was in such a state.

'Whoa! What's going on?' he cried. 'You look like you're trying to escape!'

I promptly burst into hysterical tears. I couldn't stop and it made breathing almost impossible.

'Oh, love, come here.' And Dad scooped me up into a familiar hug and kissed the top of my head. He smelled of his woody aftershave that I loved. I realized how much I had missed him and started crying even more. And I would never see Mum again. It felt like the end of the world all over again.

'Daaad, are you really going to marry Mary?!' I managed to squeak out as I pulled away from the hug.

'Oh, Daisy. Let's go and sit down. I think you and I need to have a little chat.' Oh, here we go, the 'You Need To Get Over This' speech. The 'I Am going To Marry Mary And There's Nothing You Can Do To Stop Me' speech.

We plonked down on the sofa. 'Would you like a cup of tea? And some tissues?'

'Yes, please,' I sniffled, anything to postpone what he was going to say. Looking round the room I spotted the familiar photo album that always sat on the bookshelf— containing pictures of Mum from baby to just before she died. I jumped up and slipped it out, grabbing my school bag from the hall, rooting around for the picture I'd stashed in my bra. Sitting back down I opened the album at the back—yep, no more pictures after she died. Curiously I flicked to about halfway through—I practically knew every photo by heart. I had always loved the old Eighties photos with the dreadful fashion and mad, mad hair—but looking at them now, having been there and experienced the Eighties, made the pictures come to life. Dawn with her snarly smile made me want to slap her! Mum in the prom dress we made together. Then I turned the page—there it was—the

other half of my picture: Mum gurning, me all blurry.
There was space underneath for me to fit my photos in,
to join them together. So I did—you could hardly see
the join. Looking at the picture, I remembered Mum
tickling me while I sat on her knee. An ache throbbed
in my chest. I flicked to another page and the photo of
us before the prom in Nana's back garden stared back at
me. Annie and me linking arms with Izzy and Julia, our
two faces slightly blurred so you can just about make
out who we are, but not really. I turned over a few more
pages, and instead of Dawn there were photos of Julia
with Mum. In one picture Mum is wearing the bag I'd
made strapped across her body on what looked like a
day out to Brighton. I stroked the picture gently, almost
hoping to touch Mum one last time . . .

Dad returned carrying tea and a plate of chocolate
biscuits and tissues.

'So, you're worried just because I asked you to come
on holiday that I'm going to marry Mary?'

'No. I know you're marrying Mary.' I closed the
book and took the tea.

'I'm not!'

'Well not yet, you've only just got engaged. But you'll
get married soon, won't you?'

Dad burst out laughing. 'Where has this come from?'

'The cake in the kitchen.' I started to feel like I was trotting down the wrong path.

'Daisy! Have you forgotten? Did the row yesterday frazzle your brain?' Dad was looking worried now.

'Forgotten what?'

'Tonight we're holding Uncle Jonny's surprise engagement party here. The cake is for him and Lily.' I just stared at Dad, my mouth dropping open. I had to force myself to close it again. *Uncle Jonny was getting married?* Who was Lily?

'Are you OK? What's going on, Daisy?' Dad shuffled up right next to me on the sofa. He felt my head. 'You feel very hot. Do you feel OK?'

'No. I threw up in the sink earlier, just before you came home.'

'Oh you poor thing. You must be coming down with something. Lie down here and I'll go and get a blanket. Do you want Pooh?' I nodded—I *really* wanted Pooh. Dad came downstairs and handed him to me. I felt small on the sofa covered in a blanket holding Pooh.

'Dad, I'm so sorry for the things I said about Mary yesterday. I didn't mean them.' It felt good to get that off my chest after two weeks!

'I know you didn't.' He sat down by my feet. 'But I need to say sorry too. I think I'm asking too much of you regarding Mary. Let's take it a bit slower, eh? A holiday just now might be a bridge too far.'

'OK. I would like that.' I thought about what Mum had said last week when I had talked about Mary, how she wouldn't have wanted her dad to be on his own. And how maybe I could just see what happens after all, Mum said it might be OK ... 'I do want you to be happy though, Dad.'

'Oh, I'm always happy, I've got you, haven't I?' I smiled. 'Daisy, you're the single most important person in my life. Please don't ever forget that. You and me together in our little family.'

'Oh, Daaaaaaaad!' and a tide of tears streamed from my eyes.

'Hey, what is it?'

'I wish Mum was here. I miss her. I really do. She should be here.'

His face crumpled into a frown and his shoulders sagged. 'I miss her too. Every day. And of course she should be here to see her brother getting married. It's big events like this that highlight the hole she left in our lives.'

But that wasn't what I meant. I couldn't tell him the truth. I couldn't tell him she should have remembered to wear a seatbelt like I had begged her to. Why didn't she listen? It was so unfair; I just wanted her here.

'It might make you feel better if you have a rest. You've got a few hours until people arrive. Now, Mary will be at the party, but not till later. You'll be OK, won't you?' Dad looked uncertain.

I felt my tummy twist and I wanted to say no, but Mum's words stopped me. 'Yes, I promise. Don't worry.'

'Tomorrow we need to talk about why you walked out of school before the bell. I had a phone call from your form tutor—that's why I came home early.'

'Oh.'

'Don't worry, I know you're in a tizz today so we'll shelve it until then.'

'Thanks.' I didn't care about getting into trouble. Mrs Hollingdale screaming in my face didn't faze me. I felt hollowed out; I couldn't even drink my tea.

'You've got a new dress too, don't forget.' I nodded. Normally a new outfit was cause for celebration. Nothing mattered now . . .

'I've got to go and get the ice for the drinks bucket in the garden—you OK on your own for a bit?'

'Yes, sure.'

I'd been lying on the sofa in a daze clutching Pooh for a while when I heard the back door go.

'Helloooooo? Daisy? Where are you?' It was Izzy.

'I'm here.' She walked in and I took one look at her and burst into tears.

'Oh, no! Daisy, you poor thing.' She sat down and hugged me.

'She didn't come home . . .' I sobbed into her hair. 'I can't believe it.'

'I know, Mum told me. I got worried when you never replied to any of my texts.'

'I don't know what to do,' I said twisting Pooh in my hands. I didn't really remember what it felt like when Mum died, but I'm sure it was almost as bad as this. 'Nothing's changed and I want to hide from everyone coming to this stupid party.'

'I'm not surprised you do. But it might be good?'

'How? I don't care about Uncle Jonny getting married. I feel so awful.'

'But this party is your idea!' That stopped me in my tracks.

'What? *My* idea? I haven't seen Uncle Jonny for years!'

'Where's your dad?' Izzy asked, looking round apprehensively.

'He's gone to get ice for the giant champagne bucket in the garden.'

'Good. We can't talk with him here. Did he tell you anything?'

'Nothing. Do *you* know what's going on?'

'Yes.'

'Tell me. I need the distraction.' I blew my nose on a tissue, hoping that the news would lift the heavy feeling from my heart.

'Well, I got in and Mum was home—she'd had the phone call from the school. I said I brought you back because you weren't very well and forgot to sign out— sorry, I couldn't think of a good enough lie.' I shrugged; I didn't care! 'So I just acted like nothing weird had happened and she started talking about how cool it was that Jonny had finally settled down and how everyone was so pleased about the engagement and the party etc etc.'

'It's been years since I even saw Uncle Jonny in real life. Something to do with never finding his path in life or his band failing! And then when Mum died, he kind of disappeared altogether.'

'I've never even met him. Well, apart from in 1985!' Izzy exclaimed. 'So I just started asking Mum casual questions, like I was chatting. I NEVER chat with her. We don't get on. But this was different. It was . . . nice.' Her face fell. 'Oh, sorry.'

'No, don't be silly. Just because I'm sad doesn't mean you shouldn't be happy about your mum! Carry on.'

'Well, I asked her to tell me the prom story again. It really was us who got our mums together and then we inexplicably disappeared leaving the letter.' Izzy clapped her hands. 'It all worked out!'

'How did they explain us going AWOL?' I asked, making an effort. 'And what happened to Dawn?'

'There was a big investigation, but they obviously found nothing—we are officially the Biggest Mystery EVER at Sir Walter Raleigh, so our mums made a pact to name daughters after us.' Izzy laughed, looking pleased to be an official mystery. 'Mum doesn't know about Dawn. After school they never saw her again.' Izzy took a big breath. 'But this is the most exciting part! Uncle Jonny's band wrote a song about us and it went to number one!'

'Nooooo! What was it called?'

'"The Girls From Mars."' I remember now jokingly telling Dawn that we were from outer space—the Butterfly Effect at work! 'His band were well known in the Nineties.'

'Come here!' I dragged myself off the sofa and out to the hall to view Rogues' Gallery. 'Look!' I pointed at the picture of her mum and dad with Uncle Jonny.

'Oh, wow!' she breathed. 'That's one of his number one gold discs. They must have gone out celebrating.'

I nodded, the picture making sense now. Lucky Uncle Jonny—he's got his happy ending . . .

'Who's Lily?' I asked.

'She was Jonny's PA for ages. Apparently he had some wild years, it all went to his head and then one day he just stopped partying. And by the time your mum died he'd stopped for good and helped your dad and nana look after you. Her death affected him badly, so Mum said. Well, it affected her too of course, and you and your dad. Everyone, really. He met with Lily again recently and bang, they got engaged!'

'Have you met her?'

'Apparently yes and so have you obviously—but we don't know we have! Mum loves her. And so does your dad.'

Before I could ask anything more, like how Uncle Jonny changed so much, the back door opened. 'Hellooooo! Is anyone here?' It was Julia.

Chapter twenty-one
Jonny Come Home

We met Julia in the kitchen and I had to do a double take. Here she was decades later all grown up, but I could still see the awkward thirteen-year-old girl hiding in there somewhere. Mum, you were missing all this! 'Oh, there you are,' she said. 'Are you feeling any better?' I nodded. 'Good. People will be here soon—you need to get ready, Daisy.' Dad arrived in tandem with the ice and dumped it in the cleaned-out plastic garden bin on the patio.

Upstairs in my room I sat on the bed. My new outfit was all laid out ready to wear—a polka-dot yellow skater dress with pristine white Converse. I lay back on it, not caring if I crushed it. I put Pooh over my heart and a single tear squeezed out from my eye and into my hair. How was I going to get through the days?

Mum's face smiled out at me from the picture frame on my bedside table. 'I miss you,' I whispered. There was a knock on the door making me jump. 'Come in.'

'Are you OK?' Julia asked standing in the doorway. 'You still look a bit peaky.' I could feel my lip wobbling and desperately wanted to tell her everything. I shrugged instead.

'Are you still upset about your row with your dad?' I nodded. That was safe territory; I could totally pretend I was sad about that.

Julia sat down and hugged me. 'It's OK. We all say things we regret. I was never perfect when I was your age. I'm not perfect now!' I smiled weakly—if only she knew the truth!

'You don't know how happy it makes me to see you and Izzy talking again. You two are so like your mum and me. I know she would totally love the fact you guys are friends again and that you organized your uncle's party.' Julia kissed my cheek. 'You going to get dressed? Jonny will be here soon—he's going to be bowled over! You did a great job.'

I nodded reluctantly; even though I wanted to stay in my room forever, Julia's words gave me strength to get moving.

It still hadn't sunk in that I wasn't ever going to see Mum again. I glanced at her picture next to the bed as I stepped into my dress and pulled it up. But that wasn't just how I thought of her any more. I remembered her face in the photo booth, crazy and gurning, tickling me to death. I remembered her face as she screamed on the roller coaster, clutching my hand to make me feel safe. I remembered her face being concerned when I was crying in the bathroom and she comforted me. I remembered her face being excited when Jonny said his band would play and we aced the prom. I remembered her face secretly winking at me at our leaving party. I remembered her face asleep with Pooh in her bed, blissfully unaware that I loved her more than anything.

'I can do this,' I said to Pooh, kissing him. 'I can be at the party. Mum would want me to be there.' I opened the door and Izzy was just at the top of the stairs.

'I was coming to find you,' she said looking slightly worried. 'Are you OK?'

'I honestly don't know. Realizing this is it for me, no Mum, is the hardest thing. It's like someone said I was going to get loads of presents at Christmas and then on Christmas Day, there's nothing, not even a card.'

'Daisy, I know this isn't going to help now, but you have me. I was there with you. We can talk about it all the time. I met your mum; she was my friend too—we will always have that. We can keep her alive by remembering. I'll never forget our time in 1985. It was one of the happiest of my life. You have all these shared memories—

stuff you never had before. Now you can remember your mum properly; it won't be all hazy like it was before.'

My eyes filled up with tears and I grabbed Izzy's hands.

'Thank you,' I forced out, scared I was going to crack up. 'Izzy, you're the best friend. I don't deserve you after choosing Celia. I was such a rubbish person.'

'Shh, don't be silly. Let's have a fresh start.' And she hugged me.

'Yes, let's. Come on, we need to go down.'

'What's got in to you?' Nana laughed as I hugged her super tight when she arrived with Grandpa and Izzy's dad and sister.

'I'm just glad to see you.'

There were people here I didn't know—Lily's parents and some friends. I floated round in a dream-like state, impervious to the excitement about the engagement. Numb.

'Right, everyone,' Dad said in a hushed voice walking quickly from his look-out post at the living room window, 'go and hide in the garden. They're here.' We all shuffled out to the left of the patio doors, hopefully out of view from the kitchen. The doorbell rang and Dad went off to answer it. I could hear low voices murmuring in the hall.

'Oh, what's all this?' I heard a woman's voice cry, obviously spotting the food and the balloons dotted everywhere.

'Now!' Nana hissed.

'SURPRISE!' We all jumped into view on the patio. Uncle Jonny was totally gobsmacked. He looked much older and taller than he had done yesterday and his boy-band hair was all shaved off (he was obviously going bald!!!). He was also totally transformed from the faded memory I had of him all those years ago. Lily was beautiful and glamorous with long dark hair and dark skin. She burst out laughing. She was wearing a strapless grey floaty maxi-dress, chunky silver bangles, and silver hoop earrings.

Everyone was milling around them and Dad was popping corks on the champagne bottles. Izzy and I hung back. I felt like I was intruding because I didn't really know Uncle Jonny at all—how could I say congratulations? People were shaking both their hands and kissing them and Lily was showing off her ring. As champagne was handed round Uncle Jonny tapped his glass to get everyone's attention.

'Please can I say a few words?' The buzz of excited chatter died down as we waited in anticipation. 'First of all thank you so much for this surprise. We genuinely

236

had no idea—how brilliant! So thanks, Pete, for hosting.' Everyone clapped. 'I guess a lot of you thought this day would never come. *I* thought this day would never come!' Everyone laughed. 'But I met someone very special and I want to say thank you, Lily, for saying yes!' People cheered. 'Lastly, someone very dear to me is missing from all this, my sister, Annie. I miss her every day, as I know we all do. But she has left her legacy here and without Daisy, I'm not sure I would have got through the days after she died. I know Pete feels the same.' Oh, he was talking about me! 'I believe Lily has something she wants to ask you, Daisy.' And he beckoned me to come forward. I could feel my face and ears set alight, but stood rooted to the spot. Izzy gently pushed me forward and I stumbled over towards them to the edge of the patio.

'Daisy, would you do me the honour of being my bridesmaid?' Lily asked, beaming, matching dimples to Uncle Jonny's puncturing her cheeks.

Oh! I was so surprised. All of this was just too much. I didn't know how to speak! Lily looked stricken and cast a worried glance at Uncle Jonny.

'She's not going to make you wear bright pink,' he stage-whispered and winked at me, just like he'd done at our farewell dinner a few days ago. Some of the adults chuckled.

'Y-yes,' I managed to stammer out. This was all so surreal. More cheering. Lily leant in to hug me. She smelled of expensive perfume.

'Thank you!' she gushed. 'I was so nervous just then; I thought you were going to say no!'

I shook my head, and felt majorly self-conscious standing there. What do I do now? They still felt like total strangers.

'So, Small,' Uncle Jonny addressed me, my tummy flipped. That was the pet name he had called Mum in 1985! 'I believe the party was all your idea?' I stared hard into his face, searching for the familiar Jonny from over thirty years ago. 'Thanks!' And he hugged me, not some uncomfortable uncle hug, but a proper, 'I Know Who You Are' hug. Like it came from Dad.

'Come over here, I want to tell you something.' Everyone had resumed their party chatter and he drew me over to Mum's tree in the garden. Dad had planted it a year after she'd died. A wicker heart hung off the lowest branch.

'I've never told you this before, but back in the day a wise girl once gave me some good advice. Pretty ridiculous because she was just a kid, but she told me I should never ever forget my family. I wandered off that path for a while.' He paused and looked shamefaced.

'But when you came along, all the fame and money just seemed so pointless. Seeing Annie hold you for the first time triggered that memory and I remembered what she'd said. I didn't want to miss out on you growing up.' I was gobsmacked. The Butterfly Effect in action! I felt like all the years melted away and I was standing with Jonny in Nana's living room in 1985.

'What I'm trying to say is just because I'm getting married doesn't mean you're going to get rid of me. I'm still going to be here, getting on your nerves and forcing you to come to the cinema with me.' I smiled at him and felt like something shifted inside me. 'So I know I said no bright pink, but I thought you'd look good in a peach meringue?' He raised his eyebrows.

'No!' I cried.

'OK, salmon pink? A bit of a compromise?' He winked again and for a split second I could have sworn he looked just like Mum.

'You're a salmon!' I giggled shyly.

'No, you are! Come here, Small. You've just made an old man very happy.' And he kissed my head. 'Salmon pink it is!' he whispered in my ear. 'I'm going to get something to eat. Do you care to join me, fair maiden?'

'In a sec, I think I'm just going to sit here for a moment.'

'OK, I'll try and save you something but I can't promise. I'm starving!' He wandered back to his party and I sat down under the tree, the heart scraping the top of my head. I felt different. I felt like Dorothy in the *Wizard of Oz*. Everything had been black and white, but now I could feel colour seeping back into my life. Mum might not be here, which felt like the most unfair thing in the world, but for the first time I looked around and noticed all the things I did have. Uncle Jonny wasn't a stranger, he was part of our family. And I had Dad and Julia, and my best friend, Izzy, back in my life too. And Izzy was right, I had concrete memories of Mum and someone to share them with. I'll never forget those two weeks as long as I live. Missing Mum was going to be so hideous but sitting here under her tree I felt a kind of peace that I'd not thought possible a few hours ago. I sat very still breathing in the smell of summer when a pair of trainers came into view.

'How you feeling?' Dad asked.

'OK.' He crouched down and crawled under the branches to join me.

'This tree has grown a lot in the last year. I never used to be able to sit under it.' I nodded. 'Do you fancy coming back to the party? Julia made pavlova; I know how much you love it.'

'Yes, come on then.' Dad shuffled out awkwardly and turned round and offered me his hand, hauling me up.

'Well done for this party, Daisy. I'm so proud of you. Your mum would be too.'

'Thanks, Dad.' Instead of feeling bereft when he said this, I felt almost OK. Almost OK was a good place to start.

As we made our way across the lawn towards everyone else, I felt that it was going to be all right. And one thing was for certain—there's no place like home.

Acknowledgements

First of all I would like to thank Clare Whitston at Oxford University Press for cajoling the book out of me a draft at a time. Also her team of Debbie Sims and Gill Sore — thanks for your input. Thanks to Charlie (Chiz) Viney my agent for being down with the kids and a proper gangsta, and my two friends who bolster me up through rewrites and writer's block — Vicki Hillman and Nicola Markham. You two girls have heard everything ten times over. And special thanks to Vicki and her mum, Annie, whom the characters in the book are based on. Vicki let me use her daughter's name, Daisy, for my main character. Lastly, Sharon Boxall was my main contributor for Eighties fashion that I had forgotten all about (due to trauma sustained from such bad taste and tight collars). Thanks for reminding me about lethal shiny white stilettos!

About the Author

Jess has worked as a book-seller, children's books editor, and DJ with her best friend (under the name, 'Whitney and Britney'). She spent her childhood making comics and filling notebooks with stories. Jess lives in London and draws constant inspiration from her three brilliant children!

Quiz

You won't know this because you are all way too young (me too, ha ha!!!) but I named each chapter after a song from 1985, the year Daisy and Izzy go back in time to. See if you can match the song titles on these pages to the Eighties artists who sang them overleaf. Don't cheat and ask a grown up, see if you can do it on your own then check the answers on the next page.

Love Jess x

Chapter one: Separate Lives

Chapter two: Trapped

Chapter three: You Spin Me Round

Chapter four: Road to Nowhere

Chapter five: Take On Me

Chapter six: Back in Time

Chapter seven: Everybody Wants to Rule the World

Chapter eight: Holding Out For a Hero

Quiz continued...

Here are the artists all jumbled up in no particular order. One of them has two songs in the list, but which one?:

Duran Duran

Simple Minds

Fine Young Cannibals

Glenn Frey

Colonel Abrams

Bruce Springsteen

Bonnie Tyler

Phil Collins and Marilyn Martin

Howard Jones

Survivor

Julian Lennon

A-ha

Dead or Alive

Sting

Huey Lewis and the News

Talking Heads

Phil Collins

Wham!

Bryan Adams

Tears For Fears

Quiz answers!

Chapter one .... Separate Lives, Phil Collins
and Marilyn Martin

Chapter two .... Trapped, Colonel Abrams

Chapter three .... You Spin Me Round, Dead or Alive

Chapter four .... Road to Nowhere, Talking Heads

Chapter five .... Take On Me, A-ha

Chapter six .... Back in Time, Huey Lewis and
the News

Chapter seven .... Everybody Wants to Rule the World,
Tears For Fears

Chapter eight .... Holding Out For a Hero, Bonnie Tyler

Chapter nine .... The Wild Boys, Duran Duran

Chapter ten .... If You Love Someone,
Set Them Free, Sting

Chapter eleven .... Glory Days, Bruce Springsteen

Chapter twelve .... Things Can Only Get Better,
Howard Jones

Chapter thirteen .... The Search is Over, Survivor

Chapter fourteen .... Everything She Wants, Wham!

Chapter fifteen .... One More Night, Phil Collins

Chapter sixteen .... Don't You Forget About Me,
Simple Minds

Chapter seventeen .... Summer of 69, Bryan Adams

Chapter eighteen .... The Heat Is On, Glenn Frey

Chapter nineteen .... Life in One Day, Howard Jones

Chapter twenty .... Too Late For Goodbyes,
Julian Lennon

Chapter twenty-one ..... Jonny Come Home,
Fine Young Cannibals

ALSO BY
JESS BRIGHT

Willow's life is turned upside down when she meets her dad for the first time and discovers she has a family she knew nothing about, including a half-sister who is seriously ill and needs a bone marrow transplant to survive. Is Willow brave enough to help the sister she's never known and open up her world to a whole new family?

Ready for more great stories?

Try one of these . . .

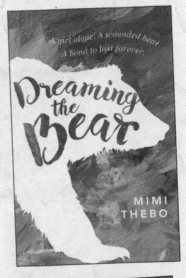